A GRIM SEARCH

A little over an hour later, by my calculation, I found the gully. After taking a long look at the surrounding country, I scuttled down the slope and made my way into the bushes. There I found a broad area of tramped dirt, some of it with grass showing through. After kicking around for a moment, I figured someone had dug two holes and piled the loose dirt between them. I had a hunch I would find Grimes in one of the two depressions.

I stood facing the area with my back to the north, where the inn would be. Someone coming from that direction would probably have buried a body with its head to the south. And he would probably lay out two bodies the same way. I decided to try the left hole first. I took out the tin plate, got down on my knees, and started scraping dirt. . . .

RAVEN SPRINGS

JOHN D. NESBITT

LEISURE BOOKS NEW YORK CITY

For Casey Fortune and all the good horses.

A LEISURE BOOK®

May 2007

Dorchester Publishing Co., Inc.
200 Madison Avenue
New York, NY 10016

ISBN-10: 0-8439-5804-9
ISBN-13: 978-0-8439-5804-1

The name "Leisure Books" and the stylized "L" with design are trademarks of Dorchester Publishing Co., Inc.

Printed in the United States of America.

Visit us on the web at www.dorchesterpub.com.

RAVEN SPRINGS

CHAPTER ONE

Raven Springs, from the first time I heard the name, sounded like a place where large, dark birds fluttered down for a drink of water after a hard day of pecking on dead flesh. As a place name, it shouldn't have been any different from others in the area—Rock Springs, Warm Springs, Hawk Springs—but it's hard to shake an image once it makes an appearance. In my mind I could see the ravens, just as I could see their cousins whenever I picked the name Buzzards Roost off a map. Hulking birds, settling like the shades of night, then croaking in an undertone as they shifted from one foot to another, holding a stiff wing halfway out for balance.

In the old Scottish songs, ravens pecked out the bonny blue eyes of a prince killed by treachery. From what I had seen in my own day, they did lower-class work. They plundered the kidneys of a jackrabbit or feasted on a gut pile left by hunters, then floated in to the water hole. That was the picture I had for the name of a place I had never been, a place I was headed towards to see if I could find a person I didn't really care for.

It all began on a pleasant day in late summer, when life had settled down to the simple, harmless task of sorting out chile peppers with a couple of my friends in Mexican town. Chanate and his wife Tina had a walled-in patio area about twenty feet square, paved with adobe, and most of it was covered with drying peppers. Not having any work that paid wages, and minding the main chance of a good meal, I thought I had just the right employment in putting the long slender chiles into one pile, the short fat ones in another, and the long thick ones in yet another. It was cramped work, crouching and kneeling and trying not to mash any peppers, but it was as mindless as a person could hope for. Even Chanate, poking a harvest needle and pulling thread through the drying stem caps, looked intellectual by comparison as he sat in his chair and held his head back. Tina was sewing *ristras*, too, and between the two of them they had filed a bushel basket with strings of scarlet peppers. When Tina got up to take the basket into the house, Chanate waited until the door closed and then he asked me a question in Spanish.

"Tell me, Yimi, is it hard work to look for someone?"

Everyone on both sides of the river knew I had just done a piece of work in that line, had had my horse shot out from under me, and had not collected any wages.

"No," I said, answering in his language as I turned. "It's not hard to look for a person. But if you find him, then things can become very difficult."

"Oh, yes, that's true," he said, in the way that some people have of ratifying a statement, regardless of where it comes from, if it sounds like good general wisdom.

I stood up to straighten my back, then took a basket and filled it from one of the mounds I had piled up. I set the hamper next to Chanate's, then slid out the half-full one and filled it from the same heap. I felt like a good boy, Yimi the helper.

Chanate spoke up again. "What do you think of doing me a favor?"

"Oh, sure," I said, though I didn't know if it had to do with the peppers or his earlier question. "What is it?"

"I need to pick up some rope at the hardware store. I told Quico I would tend to it, and they're supposed to have it ready."

"Oh." Quico lived quite a ways out, and sometimes when he came to town he killed animals for his uncle. This would be Chanate's way of returning a favor. "Do you want me to go pick it up and bring it here?"

"If it can be done."

"I'd say so." I imagined carrying back fifty feet of rope coiled up like a lariat. "Do you want me to go now?"

"It would be all right."

"Do I have to pay?"

"No, I'll settle the account later, after Quico gives me the money."

"Very well," I said. I brushed off the knees of my pants, adjusted my hat, gave a nod, and set out.

At the hardware store, I was met by a fellow in his forties, a man with a rough complexion and a large bushy head. We more or less knew each other on sight, but I hadn't ever bought anything in his store.

When he asked me how he could help me, I told him in Spanish that I was there to pick up a rope for Chanate.

"Oh, yes. Rope." He took a slip of paper off the counter and looked at it, then called out to someone named Rodrigo. A young man in his twenties came out from the dark back area of the store. "Listen," said the older man, still in Spanish. "We need to measure this rope for Chanate." He handed him the slip.

The young man, who had a clear, open face and combed-back hair, raised his eyebrows and then looked at me. "Two hundred meters and a hundred meters?"

I shrugged. "Whatever Chanate asked for."

The older man nodded.

Rodrigo walked across to the opposite wall, where large spools of rope hung crosswise on an iron frame. The young man pulled out a few yards of slack from a spool of half-inch hemp rope. Then he took his end to a nearby counter and measured off one meter at a time till he came to fifty. Next he kinked the rope, measured back another fifty against the first length, then back again two more times until he had a huge pile on the floor. Holding his thumb on what I assumed was the two-hundred-meter mark, he took the rope to the wall and cut it on a stationary triangular blade that was forged to the iron rack. Then he handed the rope, in double strands, to the older man, who worked it into a large coil. When they had it all stacked, Rodrigo cut off a couple of hanks of jute twine, and the two men tied the coil snug.

I was thinking about how much work it was going to be to carry that heap of rope back to Chanate's butcher shop, when Rodrigo went to another spool and started pulling off a length of the rope one size smaller, which I guessed to be three-eighths. He measured the first fifty meters the same way he did before, and then when he came to measure the second fifty against the first, he looped the two strands at a time from thumb to elbow, with his forearm upright. This would be the other hundred he mentioned. Again he cut the rope on the blade, which I now thought might be the tooth of a sickle bar. He tied off this coil with twine also, and he set it next to the larger pile on the counter.

I had no idea how I was going to get all that rope back to Chanate's place. As the two men were positioning the whole purchase on a scale, I recalled that these people bought and sold rope by weight even though they measured it by length.

"How much?" I asked.

"Twenty-five kilos and a half."

About fifty-six pounds, I figured. The two coils would make an awkward load to carry together in front of me, and they would be way off balance if I tried to haul one in each hand. "Do you have a burlap bag?" I asked.

Rodrigo disappeared into the dark for a minute and came back with a large new grain sack, coarse-textured and bright as wheat straw. He and I got the big heap and the little heap settled into the bag, and he gave me a nod that signified we were done. I twisted the burlap neck, hefted the load, and swung it onto my back.

"*Mucho bulto*," he said. Quite a bulk.

I winked at him and nodded. Then leaning forward, I headed for Chanate's place.

I think I might have felt conspicuous going down

the street that way if I had been on the other side of the river, where everyone could see what Jimmy Clevis had come to now that he didn't have a horse. But over here on this side I think I looked pretty normal, just another man bent over hauling a burden.

I dropped the bag so that it stood up straight in Chanate's courtyard. "Pretty heavy," I said. I thought Tina was giving it a curious look, as if she expected a midget to crawl out of it, so I turned to Chanate and asked, "What does Quico want with so much rope?"

"Oh, they always have a use for it at the ranch, and out at the sheep camp."

"I'm sure." I didn't really mind it, now that I had the job done and could relax my cramped muscles. And I always liked Quico. He was a straight-up, go-ahead young fellow. "When does he come?"

"Tomorrow."

"That's good. And how is he?"

"Fine."

"And Fernando?" I didn't care so much for Fernando, but he was Quico's *compañero*, so that was good enough. And the only time I ever saw him was when he came here with Quico.

"Fine, I hope."

"Does he come with Quico?"

"Not this time, I don't think. He's gone."

Tina rose from her chair and said she was going to fix dinner.

I took it as a good sign, as I had been having optimistic thoughts about food for well over an hour.

"Sit down," said Chanate. "Rest a little."

I sat in Tina's chair and moved my head to each side, to stretch my neck and shoulder muscles.

"This Fernando, he went away about a month ago."

"Oh, really? Is he coming back?"

"He should have returned by now."

"I see. Is anyone worried?"

"Maybe a little. He went up to Wyoming, to a sheep camp there, and no one has heard a word from him."

"Did he go to visit?"

"He took the Virgin with him."

I frowned. The only woman I knew him to have an interest in was a blonde girl I had gotten into some trouble over, and she was no virgin.

"A figure." Chanate held his left hand palm up and his right hand a foot above it, palm down.

"Oh, yes," I said, embarrassed that I hadn't caught his meaning sooner. "A little statue."

"*Ándale*. The Virgin. He was taking it to a sheep camp, where the men have a sanctuary."

I nodded. I could picture one of those shrines, candles flickering in the alcove of a dark room. "Did he arrive at the ranch?"

Chanate shook his head. "After two weeks and not hearing anything, we sent don Mauricio's son with a letter. The sheepherders told him Fernando never came."

"That doesn't sound good."

"No, not at all. We think we should do something more."

"You and Quico?"

"The people from the town will help. A small co-operation. A woman from here sent the Virgin to be paid for, and Fernando took it in good faith. No one likes the idea that they just disappear."

"With good reason." I looked over at the sack of

rope, still standing upright. "What do you think you'll do?"

"A man here in the town, Justo Salinas, knows of a man who looks for lost people."

"Has someone been in contact with him, then?"

"Yes. He is supposed to come today, more or less at this time."

It sounded like a possibility. I imagined a Mexican version of a bounty hunter, maybe wearing an old Spanish cloak and carrying a long rifle, Taos-style. But I didn't have a comment, so I waited for Chanate to speak again.

"I was hoping you might help with the translating."

"Oh, is he a gringo?"

"A North American, yes. And you know, with this kind of business, it is best to have a very good understanding."

"Of course."

"And you speak his language."

I laughed. "You never know what kind of person you might have to deal with. But it shouldn't be difficult."

"We appreciate it very much."

"A very small thing. I'll be glad to do it." Provided, I thought, that he doesn't hold up dinner for two hours.

Not long after that, a knock sounded at the courtyard gate. Thinking it might be the hunter of lost people, I got up to go answer it. When I was halfway there the gate opened, and in came Magdalena.

My pulse jumped as it always did when I saw her. She was wearing a tan dress, red lipstick, and red earrings. Her dark hair hung loose to her shoulders.

"*Buenas tardes, Yimi. Ya estás aquí.*" Good afternoon, Jimmy. You're already here.

"Yes, Nena, I am."

She gave me her hand, and her green eyes met mine. Then she turned to her uncle. "*Buenas tardes, tío.*"

I stepped aside and motioned for her to sit in the chair.

"Have you been helping?" she asked, still in Spanish, as she took a seat.

"Oh, yes." Since I had come at her suggestion to begin with, I felt I was answering to my duty.

She looked around, found Tina's needle stuck in the spool of thread, and took up the work. She threaded the needle on the first try, pulled the length through, and bit off the long strand to separate it from the spool. "And how goes it?" she asked, raising her glance and smiling.

"I was resting for a minute. Your uncle sent me to bring some rope."

"We are waiting for the stranger," said Chanate. "The man who looks for lost people."

"Oh, yes." She turned her green eyes to me again. "Then you know about Fernando, that he disappeared?"

"Your uncle told me."

"And what do you think?"

"It seems to me that if a man didn't show up where he was supposed to, things aren't in the right order. But it's good that someone is going to do something."

"Oh, yes. That's true." She looked at Chanate. "And when does the man come?"

"We expect him pretty soon. Yimi says he will translate."

"That's very good," she said, smiling. "Nobody makes a fool out of Yimi. Isn't that right, Yimi?"

I laughed. "I imagine everyone is a fool for something at some time. But your presence will give me courage." I waited for her to laugh, and then I went on. "I'm curious to see what this stranger looks like and to hear what he says."

I didn't have to wait long. Nena had no more than a dozen chiles strung on her *ristra* when a knocking came at the gate. I looked at Chanate and asked him where he wanted to have the conversation.

"Here in the *zaguán*," he said, meaning the patio or courtyard.

Nena set her work on top of the basket of chiles, rose from her chair, and said she would go help her aunt with the meal.

The knock came again as I walked toward the gate. When I opened it, a Mexican boy about twelve years old stood there. A few feet in back of him slouched a man who could be none other than the man we were expecting.

"*Hola, Yimi,*" said the lad in a rush of Spanish. "Comes here an American who wishes to speak with don Chanate."

"He's here inside. I can introduce the man."

The boy turned to leave, and the stranger stepped forward, brushing past him.

"*Gracias, Artemio,*" I said. Then to the visitor, "Come on in." As he came up to me I held out my hand and said, "I'm Jimmy Clevis."

"Name's Milaham," he said as he shook my hand. "Ross Milaham."

I took him in at a glance. He wore a flat-crowned, flat-brimmed hat that shaded his face but did not hide a milky left eye. Straight brown hair hung down over his ears, and a week's stubble gave a seedy texture to his face. As he passed through the door ahead of me, I saw a cluster of boils on his neck.

I followed him inside and introduced him to Chanate, then stood back and took his measure again. He wore a sackcloth coat and a pair of denim trousers, neither of which fit him very well. I had the impression that the two garments, earlier in life, had belonged to two other people. I could see the tip of a holster poking below the hem of his coat, and I had already seen him pat the sackcloth a couple of times. I imagined he did so to make sure his gun was in place, but I sensed that men sometimes made those gestures as a way of letting others know that here was a man who went armed. He didn't seem like the type who would scruple much about using a weapon on another person, and I wouldn't have been surprised to know that he had a knife tucked away somewhere.

We began the interview with Chanate saying that he understood the gentleman had a line of work in which he looked for people. Milaham said he did, and Chanate went on to give a general account of how and when Fernando disappeared. Then he asked if it was the kind of case that the gentleman took on.

"It might be," said Milaham to me. "You don't have to tell him all of this, but I don't bother much with Nagurs or Indians or Chinamen. A Meskin, though, he's kind of on the borderline. Is this fella worth anything?"

"Do you mean the lost man?" I answered.

"Yeh. What I mean is, was he carryin' money and

on a serious kind of bidness, and not the kind to fall into drinkin' and playin' cards and just gettin' himself stabbed by some other Mexicans?"

I relayed the question and brought back the answer, to the effect that Fernando always went well dressed, was a serious kind of man, and whether he had a little money or more than that, would be careful with whatever he did. He went to the dances and the rooster fights just like anyone else, but he would have stuck to business on this trip.

Milaham wrinkled up his nose and said, "I s'pose I could do it. Give it a try. I'd have to have a pitcher, though."

"A picture?"

"Yeh." He reached inside his coat and brought out a large greasy wallet, which he then held open in his left hand. With his right he ruffled through a sheaf of drawings and photos. He showed a drawing of a fat man with a bulldog face, then a photo of a girl with a gap in her teeth. He lifted the corners of a few others to give us an idea of his variety. "Somethin' to go on," he said. "You cain't expect me to just go look for a Meskin and that's it. Just about everyone I ask, they'll tell me they all look the same. So I need a pitcher. Somethin' to show."

"I see." I conveyed that information to Chanate, who raised his eyebrows and then moved his head up and down. I said to our visitor, "It looks as if you keep a lookout for several people at the same time."

"Oh, yeh. Kill two birds with one stone. And thet way, no one has to put up too much money to begin with."

"I understand. And how much would that be in a case like this?"

"Fifty just to carry his pitcher, fifty if I find 'im, and then anythin' else it costs me."

"Such as?"

"Some people's mouths stay pretty tight until they see a shiny little piece of silver or gold." He tipped his head back with a knowing air, poked his cheek out with his tongue, and seemed to look down at me with his good eye. The other one, I noticed, seemed to wander on its own track.

"Of course." I shared Milaham's information with Chanate, who looked at his feet and nodded.

"It's difficult," he said. "We would have to get a picture. And the man doesn't put himself out to look for only one person."

"It doesn't seem like it."

"It's difficult," he said again. "I doubt that anyone has a drawing or a photo. I know we don't have anything."

I had the impression that Chanate didn't care much for the stranger's style but was putting his hesitation in terms of the picture. I turned to Milaham, who was folding his wallet and making ready to put it away. "I think we might have a problem with getting a likeness," I said.

"Happens all the time. You'd be surprised how many people don't leave a trace. Comes a time like this, and no one so much as has a sketch of 'em." He glanced at Chanate. "But if he wanted me to, I could get started on it now, and get the pitcher later."

"You mean put some money down today."

"That's right. And I'll be comin' through here again in about a month. I could get the pitcher then."

I conferred with Chanate and came back with the

answer. "He thinks it would be better to wait until we have the picture."

Milaham shrugged. "That suits." He had put away the wallet, and now he patted the skirt of his coat where it covered his gun. "I'll be back in a month or so, and if he wants, we can do business then." After we had thanked him and had shaken hands around, he lifted his nose and sniffed. "Smells like good grub comin' up." He smiled without showing his teeth.

When the gate closed and we heard the hoofbeats clopping away, Chanate raised his eyebrows and said, "Maybe he has a good nose for some things, like the coyote, but I don't think he is the best for us."

"What do you think is next, then?"

"Well, to eat. Don't you think? Then we'll see."

I was happy to be seated again at Chanate and Tina's table, beneath the painting of the Last Supper, which always seemed like such a wholesome influence. The meal itself was worth the wait, and I felt no shame at having three servings of pork and red chile, plus frijoles and tortillas. When the meal was done I thanked Tina, who thanked God, and then the rest of us thanked God as well. Tina and Nena cleared the table and withdrew into the kitchen. As the clatter of dishes came from the kitchen, Chanate set down his toothpick and took a breath.

"Well, what did you think of the American?"

"Like you, I didn't think he would dedicate himself to the job very well."

"And what did you think of the job itself?"

"Of looking for Fernando? I think it could be a

normal job or perhaps a very difficult one. One would find out."

"I think so. And yet we need someone to do it."

"Well, yes."

He paused, a serious look on his dark face. "Do you think it is something you could do?"

"I don't know." I had been expecting the question, just as I had been wondering at what point he had decided to try me on it. I thought he might have been considering me all along and was hoping not to have to ask me. Even so, at this point he had to, and I felt that I couldn't very well say no. "I suppose I could do it, but I don't even have a horse."

"Oh, we can get you a horse."

I shrugged. "I imagine I can take a trip up that way. Wyoming, you said. When we were talking with the wall-eyed man you said it was near Rawlins, didn't you?"

"Yes."

"Do you have any idea of what kind of a horse you might find for me?"

"Quico said he was going to bring a little black horse into town."

I smiled at him. "How long ago did you have me picked for this job?"

He shrugged. "We had to talk to your compatriot first, but I told Quico it would be a good idea to bring a horse just in case we needed it." He made it sound simple, and maybe it was. "I had my doubts about that other man from the beginning."

"But not about me."

"Oh, we like you too much."

CHAPTER TWO

On the other side of the river, in the part of town that I thought of as the white side, I kept to the shade as I walked along the main street. The sun was still keeping the afternoon warm, but it had slipped enough in the sky that it cast shadows beyond the sidewalk. For me, the sun over the yardarm also meant that it was late enough in the day for me not to feel guilty about slipping into the Jack-Deuce.

By this time of the afternoon I could usually find Tom Devlin there. He was an older fellow who seemed to know a little about everything, and I found him more interesting to talk to than some of the louts that hung around barrooms. We also had friends in common. He knew the folks on the Mexican side of town, went to their dances, and spoke his version of their language. They called him "Tome," which in English would rhyme with "home," and they had respect for him because of his age and knowledge. If his name came up in conversation, someone was likely to say, "Oh, yes, Tome. He is very good. He knows many things." So I thought that in addition to quaffing a cool beer, I might see if Tome knew anything about the country I was planning to travel through.

I crossed the street in the bright sunlight and went in through the front door. I knew it would seem dark inside, so I paused and looked into a corner to let my eyes adjust. As far as habits went, it was not a bad one. I went to the bar, called for a glass of beer, and looked around. Tome was sitting at a table with a man I didn't recognize, but that didn't surprise me. Tome was a free spirit, as he said of himself. He owed nothing to anyone, and he associated with whatever company struck his fancy. Strangers often ended up at his table.

When he waved to me, I took my glass over to his table and sat down. The other man looked my way and nodded, then went on talking. I gathered that he and Tome were having a conversation about smuggling. As my gaze traveled back and forth between them, I noted what a contrast they made—the stranger, large-featured and portly with a wet lower lip sticking out, and Tome, slender and neat in his spectacles, trimmed gray hair, and Vandyke beard, and with a general dryness about his closed mouth. The large man had two glasses of beer in front of him, while Tome had a glass of whiskey, a tobacco pouch, and his briar pipe.

When the other man paused to take a swallow of beer, Tome spoke up. "Let me make some introductions. This is Jimmy Clevis, a young man of many talents. And this is Mr. Entwistle— Roderick Entwistle, if I caught it right."

During Tome's introduction, I took the opportunity to get a better look at the man. It seemed as if he tried to dress well, but he had a general film on him from not having bathed lately and not having had his clothes laundered, although he didn't look as if he would have done much physical labor to get them dirty. He hadn't shaved for a day or two, and from what I saw of the brown hair crawling out beneath the short-brimmed hat, he hadn't washed his head for at least a week. His jacket was coming unsewn at the hem, and a button was missing on his spreading waistcoat.

Mr. Entwistle nodded, then looked straight at me and smiled. "A man of many talents, heh? What's your line of work?"

"I tend to think of myself as a ranch hand, but sometimes I take on other jobs."

He gave me a close look, and his lower lip seemed to stick out even further. "Indeed? What kind?"

"Oh, just a little while ago I fetched a bundle of rope for a man."

Mr. Entwistle made a slight frown, as if he was disappointed that I didn't declare myself a breaker of wild horses or an exterminator of cattle thieves.

Tome's voice came up in a cheerful tone. "If there's a pretty girl around, you might well find him cranking a butter churn or stirring a laundry tub."

Mr. Entwistle smiled now and gave forth a jolly little laugh. "You'll do fine, my boy."

"Thanks," I said. "And yourself, what kind of work do you do?"

He paused, as if he didn't like the question coming from me, and then he said, "I handle correspondence for a man named Horace Finney. Perhaps you know of him. Mines, timber, and some cattle."

"Oh, yes." I had heard of the man, all right, and not always in the most glowing terms. "Are you a secretary, then?"

The term seemed to ruffle his dignity. "Not quite."

I had known of lots of men who were secretaries, and some of them with good-paying positions, so I wondered if it was the word itself. "More like a stenographer, then? I knew a fellow who did that kind of work, and he could bang out pages on a typewriting machine, straight from a set of notes that looked like fish hooks and tangled horsehair."

"I wouldn't call myself that either, with all respect to your friend."

"Not at all," said Tome. "A person in the employ of a person of wealth, influence, or great intellect deserves a loftier term. Like 'amanuensis.' That's what the great blind poet Milton had." He looked at me. "After all, a stenographer has to take down the words of blackmailers, thieves, and murderers." He made a backward wave with his hand. "I express no judgments, of course. I'm sure those people have interesting things to say." He turned to Mr. Entwistle. "But an amanuensis would follow the discourse of one person. I secretly suspect that your employer is a fugitive from a foreign court and that, under cover of writing correspondence about his chattels, you are taking down a long document of self-vindication."

Mr. Entwistle bubbled out another laugh. "I think you've found me out."

With his earlier laugh I thought he was putting on

the jolly humor of the well-fed person, but now I sensed that it was the humor of the person who has never had much luck making friends. He wanted Tome to like him.

On a hunch, and not thinking much beforehand, I asked, "Do you know a man named Milaham? Ross Milaham?"

He frowned, then shook his head. "No, not at all. That's not your stenographer friend, is it?"

"No, it's someone I met earlier in the day."

"When you were fetching rope?"

"No, it didn't have anything to do with that. He was just passing through, and I did a little translating for him over in Mexican town."

"Well, you *are* a lad of many talents, aren't you?"

Tome's dry voice came in again. "There's a butter churn over there that Jimmy would like to turn the paddles on."

Mr. Entwistle gave a broad smile. "Have at it while you're young." Then, as if he was dismissing me, he straightened his waistcoat and took another drink of beer.

Now I thought I understood him better. He would allow Tome an even footing in the conversation, but not me. Either of them could be humorous or forward, but a young pup would just as well stay in his place. I shrugged it off, assuming that sooner or later he would finish his beer and go on his way. Meanwhile I settled back in my chair and let him and Tome resume their conversation about smuggling.

Tome stuffed his pipe and lit it. "I think some people are more fit for that kind of work because of their temperament," he said. "Calm and devious, plenty of nerve."

"Physical ability counts for something, too," said the other man. "Women, for example, have always been good at smuggling jools."

"That's a talent in itself," observed Tome. "And having the right equipment."

"Yes, and there's more than one way to hide something inside. I've heard how men practice swallowing things whole. They start with grapes, then move on to small sausages. Lubricate 'em with olive oil, and get used to gettin' 'em down."

Tome gave him a nod.

"Then when they want to transport the real thing, they wrap it in a casing, force it down the same way, and pass it out a day or two later."

"Tricks of the trade."

"The only thing is, sometimes the plan fouls up. Over in Arabia or one of them places, there was a fella, a kind of spy or confidential agent, who had the job of smuggling a poison into the inner circle of some palace. He wrapped the drug in sheep gut, got it down the hatch, and went on his mission. But the wrapping didn't hold up, and the stuff broke loose inside him. Hell of a dose. Died a miserable death."

Tome blew out a stream of smoke. "It might have been better if the fellow had just poked it up his ass. Wonder if he thought of that when he saw things had gone wrong."

"Oh, he might have been told not to do it that way. Whoever was the mastermind might have thought someone would run a finger up there to check him out. Those sneaky people know one another, and the ones who wanted to get to the sultan or whatever he was would have been trying to out-think the guards."

"Too bad for him, then. He must have thought he was following good advice."

"And he might have been. But even that method, when it holds up, is no guarantee the fellow will get through. Sometimes if they think someone's carrying something, they hold 'em in a little room for a few days, and collect whatever passes through 'em. That's the nice way." He gave a knowing look as he drained the last of his first glass of beer. "In the not-so-friendly way, men have been killed just so someone could cut open their bowels and get what they were carrying. Poison or jools either one, stuffed in from top or bottom."

Tome looked at me and nodded, as if to say, "Take warnin'."

"In fact," said Mr. Entwistle, regaining the floor, "that's the routine way with animals. Get something down their throat, get 'em to where they're goin', then kill 'em and open 'em up. Simple as pie, if nothin' goes wrong."

"It *would* be a bit difficult," said Tome, "if you got a huge bolus down a mule and then he died in the middle of the street."

"Yes, or if the animal gets mistaken for another. I know of one case where some jool thieves forced the stone down a goose's throat, felt it go down the gullet, and left. Then when they came back in a few hours, they got the wrong goose. They took it home in a sack, got it out of sight, and did it in, only to find no stone. Meanwhile, the other goose got sent off to market and fell into the hands of some other people. Eventually the police tracked it down."

"The hell," said Tome.

"A true story. 'Course, there's nothin' new in this

world. If the crooks know all the tricks, so do the ones who want to catch 'em. Some of your best inspectors have the criminal mind, you know, and some of 'em have it in their blood."

"Sure," said Tome. "That's why I advise all my criminal friends to go into police work. Turn their talents to safe use. Like my young friend here," he said, pointing his pipe stem at me. "A dyed-in-the-wool forger, embezzler, and swindler. He could go to work for the government, or even the Pinkerton company. Catch some big fish that's been leechin' off the public trust. Trim him down to the fins."

Mr. Entwistle looked at me as if it was my fault Tome was making the joke. I didn't think he resented me for being an improbable forger, but I thought he had a glimmering that Tome was making fun of his employer, as that was the way I took it, and I sensed that he didn't like me being part of the audience. "Maybe some bluegill," he said.

The conversation didn't pick up after that. Mr. Entwistle seemed to have lost his interest in showing off his worldly knowledge, and he fell into something of a sulk. I took advantage of the lull and asked Tome how things had been.

"Same as always," he said. "Work and church."

I laughed. As far as I knew, the hardest work Tome ever did was carry the newspaper home. Common knowledge had it that he had sold some family property a few years back and kept his needs modest. And as for church, I don't think he even went to funerals, and if he went to any weddings it would be over in Mexican town, where he would be on the lookout for *viudas* and *solteronas*.

"How about yourself?" he said.

"Oh, I spent most of the day across the river."

"And how's everything there?"

"Well enough."

Our portly visitor didn't seem to enjoy being marginal to the conversation. He drank down his second glass of beer and took leave, thanking us for the company.

When he was gone, I told Tome I thought this fellow Entwistle had some good stories.

"It would seem so. Hard to say how he came by them."

"I thought the one about the mistaken identity of the goose was interesting."

"He said it was a true story, and it might have been at one time. But I'm quite sure I read it in a detective story a few years back. Something about a blue carbuncle. And the other story, about the smuggler in Arabia, probably came from some old tale like 'Ali Baba and the Forty Thieves.' That's what happens. These stories go from one teller to the next, and before long someone is willing to swear it's a true story. They must think it has more weight that way. Makes them seem more knowledgeable. As long as he was holding forth, he was happy."

"He seemed to think your joke about the stenographer was funny. I know I did."

"Oh, I have to admit, I borrowed the skeleton of it from a famous anecdote. Doctor Johnson, the lion of the eighteenth century, is said to have quipped to another man that 'under cover of running a bawdy house, your wife is actually a receiver of stolen goods.'"

I laughed. "That's pretty good."

"Yes, it is. Better than mine. In addition to being shorter, it has more wit, but we take what we can."

"He didn't seem to appreciate your last joke, though, about me being an investigator of fraud."

Tome looked at his glass. "Maybe the borrowed jokes are better. Like the stories." He swirled the whiskey, then took a sip. "Anyway, you were starting to tell me what was new in Mexican town before our visitor got up and left."

"Oh, yeah. Well, I guess the main news is that a fellow named Fernando has turned up missing."

"Fernando. The tall one, comes to town with Keekoe, always scrubbed and neat as a pin?"

"That's the one."

"Well, what happened to him?"

"No one knows for sure, it seems. He went off to Wyoming, up by Rawlins, to take a figurine of the Virgin to some fellas at a sheep camp, and he disappeared somewhere along the way."

"Just vanished in thin air?"

"No one knows. But they sent a young man up there when he didn't come back, and according to the story, Fernando never showed up at the sheep camp."

"That doesn't sound good."

"That's what I said."

"A fellow like him, a serious type, he's not the kind to dilly-dally around at the roadhouses, especially if he's on an errand like that. They take their saints and virgins pretty serious."

"Sure. And he's been gone for about a month."

"That's way too long to lay up at a whorehouse. I don't think even you could last that long."

"Not on my wages."

"So what's your guess, from what they said?"

"No tellin'. But they want someone to go up there and look around. They were going to see about this fellow I translated for, Milaham, but he didn't seem like a very good prospect. So Chanate asked me if I would do it."

"Huh. That's what you get for not having anything better to do. What do you think about it?"

"Well, I said I would do it. The *gente* over there got together a little collection, I guess, to pay the expenses."

"Better they give it to you than to Molohan."

"Milaham."

"Huh," he said. "How long do you figure you'll be gone?"

"Maybe a couple of weeks. Get back before the weather turns cold."

He nodded as he rotated his drink glass.

"By the way," I said. "Do you know anything about the country up there?"

"Nothin' to speak of. Range land, cattle and sheep. Bad country for blizzards. Rawlins itself is a hard town, on the railroad. That's where they hung old Big Nose."

"I'll probably have to get off the beaten track as well."

"Uh-huh. You be careful wherever you go. Doesn't sound like the easiest way to make a wage."

"No, and if I was just interested in the money, I'd do something else. But the way I see it, these people need someone to go take a look, and they trust me. And for my part, I don't want to let 'em down."

"You need to think about yourself, too, you know. No need to get yourself hurt just because you think someone expects it of you."

"No, I've thought about it in my own way, and it seems like the right thing to do. I've got this task, and I want to follow through with it. If something's not right, I want to find out why."

"You're a regular crusader, aren't you?"

"No, just a fool."

"There are worse kinds."

I thought about a time, not too far back. "I guess so. Like the kind I used to be."

"Oh, well, at least you got away from that girl."

He meant the blonde girl, and I was thinking about the time when I used to throw the wide loop. I left it at that. "Well, I'll get to see some new country."

"Oh, yeah. By the way, how are you plannin' to travel? Not on foot, I hope."

"Um, no. They're supposed to fix me up with a horse. Quico's going to bring one into town."

"That doesn't sound so bad. Get you there and back. I hope you're not gone for long, of course."

"Me neither."

"I'd hate to see someone else get in there and put his hand on that butter churn. There are too many of these young sports around."

A minute earlier I had thought he might be sparing my feelings, but if he had been he hadn't weakened for long. "Thanks for the encouraging words," I said.

He gave me a sharp look through the spectacles. "You won't get 'em just any old where you go."

"I know."

* * *

On my way back to Chanate's the next day, I thought about how simple things had seemed such a short time before—how I had been content to sort chiles into little heaps, and how I had been able to abandon my mind as I walked to the hardware store. I had seen a flock of blackbirds start up from a row of elms, and I had pronounced my friend's name a few times. *Cha-na-te, Cha-na-te, Cha-na-te*. And the word for rope: *so-ga, so-ga*. All the innocence of just making sounds. Now I had to think about searching for a man who had disappeared. I couldn't take Mr. Entwistle too seriously, but all his enthusiastic talk about intrigues and palace guards and cutting open a man's bowels to get at the contraband made me worry, in a general way, about any dangers that might lurk along my route.

When I got to Chanate's butcher shop, I saw a black horse tied up outside. He was a husky, short-coupled gelding, bareback and tied with a rope halter. As I stopped to look him over, Chanate appeared in the doorway of his shop.

"Buenas tardes, Yimi."

"Buenas tardes." Then I asked, still in Spanish, "Is this the horse?"

"Yes, it is. What do you think?"

"I like him." I stepped forward, patted him on the neck, and ran the palm of my hand down the ridge of his back. "Is Quico here?"

"No, he had to go back to the ranch. But he thanks you for helping us."

"Very well." I scratched the horse on the jaw.

"Quico says they call the horse Negrito."

"Negrito." Little ... to go." I picked up a h... horseshoe, then let the forele... anything else?"

"Only that he was sorry not to be a... off. He wishes you a safe trip."

"It's all right," I said. "Short farewells are a$_b$ ee-able with me." I began to untie the halter rope from the hitching rail.

"Wait a minute! Wait a minute!"

"Oh, don't worry. I'm not leaving that fast. I wanted to walk him a little bit, to get to know him."

"Oh, all right, but don't be in such a hurry."

"I'm not in a hurry, but I have my saddle and my things ready to go, so I do expect to leave pretty soon."

"Very well. I'll be right back." He went into his shop.

I walked the little dark horse down the street a hundred yards, all the time watching his feet. I stopped and watched him come to a halt, and I liked the way he stood with his weight over his hooves. Then I walked him back to the butcher shop, where Chanate was waiting for me.

"This is a small thing," he said, as he pressed a leather pouch into my palm. "But I hope it is enough."

I smiled as I shook his hand. "Don't worry, friend. I travel light."

"Take care of yourself, and God bless you, Yimi."

"Thank you. I'll be back soon."

"*Con el favor de Dios, Yimi.*"

With the favor of God. It was not good to take an outcome for granted. "*Sí, con el favor de Dios.*"

* * *

When I had the dark horse saddled and my gear tied on in back, I had one more stop to make before I left town. I rode Negrito back across the plank bridge to Mexican town, turned left on a street I had come to know better than the others, and stopped at a little house on my right.

Nena opened the door and stepped outside, looking very much as she had the day before. I swung down from the horse and met her on the pathway.

"Are you going already, Yimi?"

"I think so. I have everything ready, and there are a few hours of daylight left."

"It's a long trip, and you, all by yourself."

"I'm used to it."

Her eyes met mine as she said, "I could go with you."

Her offer took me by surprise, and I had to give it a moment. I hated to turn down the company, but I let better judgment prevail. "I think it would be less complicated if I went by myself."

She gave me a close look. "I hope that doesn't mean there will be trouble."

"It is my intention to avoid trouble. In the first place, I want to come back and see you as soon as possible. And in the second place, I think someone owes me a beer out of all this."

"That's why we all like you so much, Yimi," she said, laying her hand on my cheek. "You have such good motives."

Then we met in a kiss, and I drew back.

"You go so quickly."

"As I said to your uncle, short farewells are agreeable with me."

"It's your custom, isn't it?"

"I imagine so. I think it's supposed to be not so sad."

"It seems cold to us, but that is your way."

I kissed her again. "Do you like my horse?"

"He's very pretty. May he carry you well."

"Thank you. I'll be back soon, Nena. *Con el favor de Dios.*"

"*Buen viaje, Yimi. Que Dios te lleve.*" Have a good trip. May God take you along.

I swung up onto the black horse, lifted my hat to Nena, and loosened the reins. Negrito took off at a lope. I turned once to wave to Magdalena, and then I was on my way to Wyoming.

CHAPTER THREE

The little dark horse Negrito brought me over the line into Wyoming toward the end of my third full day of travel. At a spot where the long downhill slope met a little creek, I turned off the trail and went upstream a quarter of a mile. I stripped the horse and set him out to graze in a grassy draw. After I gathered up a couple of armloads of firewood, I settled into my camp, built a fire, and gazed at the flames.

I had been given plenty to think about before I set off on this trip, and along the trail I had mused about Fernando's disappearance, Milaham's wallet full of lost people, and Mr. Entwistle's smugglers.

I don't mind traveling alone or being off on my own for a spell, but I have noticed that solitude can lead a fellow to see things in a narrow way. It helps to be around people, even if they aren't doing anything more than beating a rug, yanking on the lead rope of a donkey, or rolling barrels on a loading dock. A fellow sees these things, and they help him stay in touch with the everyday world. But let him get out of touch, and the world goes strange. Things that might otherwise seem odd or sinister begin to seem normal. The world becomes a place where a man carrying a figurine of the Virgin is liable to vanish in thin air and where every turn of the trail might set a person face to face with a road agent who wanted to cut him open to see if he had any diamonds in his bowels. A fellow begins to wonder how many people in the world practice swallowing sausages and whether men who look for lost people ever cheat to find them.

The whole idea of one person hiding some kind of a dingus inside him, then another person wanting to cut him open to get at it, loomed in my mind like a kind of threat against my own vulnerable body. I dismissed it as a bogey-man story, but the thought kept coming back to give me a queasy feeling.

Milaham, the scruffy stranger, also kept showing up in my daydreams. I might well have been able to put him out of my mind if I hadn't thought I saw him in Fort Collins. It was all a fleeting impression. I had paused on the street to watch a couple of men unloading blocks of ice from a wagon and carrying them into a saloon. The chunks had to weigh a good fifty pounds or more, and I found it interesting to see how a man would hook his tongs into a block, twist his torso, and then, with the tongs slung over his shoulder, stoop into the labor of hauling the cold, dead weight into the building. At one point my gaze drifted, and I thought I recognized the flat-crowned, flat-brimmed hat and sackcloth coat. Then a passing coach closed the man from view, and I did not see him again when things cleared. But it was enough to keep Milaham coming back into my thoughts.

Even as my mind drifted from one set of images to another, I kept to my purpose and the trail ahead. I tried to imagine where Fernando might be holed up if he was still alive, but I didn't know him well enough to form a picture. I conjured ideas of a person struck by amnesia, but it seemed like an explanation a person came up with when nothing else worked. I also remembered a story I had heard once from a man who said he had gone blind for three days, traveling alone, when he drank some bad water. He had to take care of his horse and mind his camp in total darkness, not knowing night from day except by the feel of the sun. I tried to imagine Fernando in some kind of situation like that, but I couldn't make it fit either.

I couldn't overlook the worst possibility, of course. Something fatal could have happened to him, either by accident or by evil intention. I didn't have a definite feeling, or presentiment, as they put it in Spanish, as to whether Fernando was dead or alive, but I didn't feel optimistic. I don't know how I might have felt if I hadn't had all those other murky thoughts crowding in, but even on a fair day I had some sense of what my fellow man was capable of. From the time I set out on this trip I had assumed I would start looking in earnest when I got to Laramie, and now that I had crossed into Wyoming, I was beginning to feel uneasy about what I might find.

* * *

I rode into Laramie on a bleak afternoon. A cold wind blew across the plain and whistled past the corners of buildings. Here and there a canvas awning flapped, and horses at the hitchracks had slewed around to take the wind at their rumps. Dust and grit carried on the air, and if a fellow had had much to smile about, his lips and teeth would have gotten peppered.

I found a trading post on the right side of the main drag. It looked like a good place to ask about travelers, so I stopped in.

The proprietor, a man with dirty gray hair and a pair of thick spectacles, stuck his tongue out of one corner of his mouth as he listened to me. He gave a slow shake of the head.

"I don't know anything, and I like to keep it that way. A lot of men come by this way. I don't ask questions, and I don't get asked many. I don't try to remember much. Mind my own business and let others do the same."

Then he straightaway asked me half a dozen questions in a row—what my name was, where I was from, where I was headed, what the weather had been like in Colorado, was I traveling light, and did I think we would have an early winter. After that he dropped back into the topic I had asked him about.

"You let on like this Mexican's some kind of a friend, but I've got a hunch that's not the whole story. Sounds to me like this fella skipped out on his friends. I hope you ketch him. If he pulls any tricks in this part of the country he'll find out what for. Like Black Ned the horse thief. One bullet on a Sunday morning, and it put an end to a lot of trouble.

Uh-huh. So don't be surprised if someone else gets to him before you do. You says he's a clean-lookin' Mexican. Well, they might be the worst kind."

I thanked him for his help and walked out into the windy afternoon. I rode through town, and after a couple of more inquiries I decided to cross the Medicine Bow Mountains rather than follow the Union Pacific route up and around the long way to Rawlins. I rode past the stone walls of the prison, which I understood was built in the territorial days and was still serving its purpose. I imagined a surly bunch of murderers, train robbers, and cattle thieves grumbling about having to eat boiled cabbage, and I was glad I had made a deliberate decision, not too far in my past, to try to avoid keeping company with those kinds of men. Even simpler, I was glad they were inside and I was out.

On the west side of town I found another roadside establishment that looked like a stopping place for travelers. The proprietor this time was a beady-eyed, sharp-nosed man wearing a Scotch cap and chewing a toothpick. He said he had no recollection of anyone answering to the description I gave him. Then on a hunch I asked him if he knew a man named Milaham.

His eyes narrowed. "I might. What's he look like?"

I gave him a description of the hat, the coat, and the one eye that didn't track with the other.

"Oh, yeh."

"Not exactly a bounty hunter, I guess. But he's in the business of looking for lost people."

"Uh-huh. He goes up and down this country. I'd say I last saw him a week, ten days ago."

"Is there any money in that kind of work?"

"Oh, there might be. Some people are willing to pay a pretty good reward. There's a doctor in Seneca, for example, whose little girl disappeared, and he's had an offer up for a few years now."

"Huh. The fellow I'm lookin' for has been gone a little over a month, and I'm afraid even his trail has gone cold in that much time."

"Could be," said the man as he shifted the tooth-pick with his tongue. "Sometimes they just take a powder."

Another day's travel took me across the windy plain, where I saw more antelope than cattle and more jackrabbits than people. At the end of the day I camped on the Little Laramie River, where I washed my face in cold water and set a camp. I hadn't made but about thirty miles that day, as I did not want to push the little dark horse too hard before we came to the mountains. As I watched the shadows stretch out, I was pretty sure we'd have some good climbs to make in the next couple of days.

In the morning I rolled up my camp and got a good start on the day. Before the sun was very high, we were following a grade up off the plain and into the timber. The weather was cool but sunny, and the wind was no more than a light breeze. Negrito was plucking right along, and I wondered if the fresh smell of the pine trees helped him pick up his feet. After about half an hour of climbing, I started look-ing for a place to give him a breather, and as my gaze wandered, something caught my eye.

About a quarter of a mile off the trail, in the shade

of a big pine, two men were pulling down on a rope that was slung over a branch. I stopped and watched. One of the men held the rope while the other led one of their horses closer. The man with the rope gave it a few turns around the saddle horn and then held the loose end as the other man tugged on the reins and pulled the horse forward. With the story of Black Ned the horsethief still recent in my memory, I half expected to see a dark human figure being hoisted aloft. To my surprise, a pair of grayish-tan hocks rose into view, and then the pale underside of a deer.

Seeing no harm in a visit, I turned my horse in their direction and ambled over. By the time I got there, the men had raised the deer so that the antlers cleared the ground, and they were tying off the rope to a smaller pine tree. In place of a singletree or gambrel, they had cut two notches in a stick, had spread the haunches with it, and had tied the rope to the middle of the crosspiece and had hauled it up that way. As the dead animal rotated, stopped, and twisted back the other way, I saw that it had a neat three-point rack on each side.

One of the men moved to the deer to hold it still. Its back and right side were in view, and I could see a red splotch on its ribs.

"Looks like you got a nice buck," I said, hoping to start off on a cheery note.

The man grabbed the deer's tail and pulled it down and around. "This is a doe!" he said, in what sounded like an accusing tone.

I looked again at the antlers and then at the bare crotch. "Huh. Must be some kind of a freak."

"Hermaphrodite," announced the other man,

who had taken out a sheath knife and was moving toward the deer. He made it sound as if they had killed the deer for that reason, but I was sure they had shot at it because it had antlers. It would have been hard to see what it had between its legs.

As for the word he used, I had heard it on the farm, and I understood it to mean having both male and female parts. A few years later, at a circus, I paid good money to see what I thought would be a human, but all of us in line were led through a tent where a man had a fat black dog on its side on a table and held its hind legs apart. I was too ashamed to look at details, and most of the other people seemed embarrassed, too. They just walked out the back side of the tent, shaking their heads. All the same, I was pretty sure the dog fit the definition of the word as I had learned it.

I saw no need to point that out to these fellows, though, as they didn't seem inclined to want to discuss it. Rather, I thought they wanted to blame someone or something for the oddity.

"I imagine it'll eat the same," I said.

The man with the knife answered. "Don't know as I'd want to eat any of it, now that I see what it is. But the skin's worth somethin', and we can take a look inside while we're at it."

I didn't feel invited to stick around for the autopsy, so I laid the rein against Little Blackie's neck and touched him with the spur. "Well, good luck to you," I said.

"Same to you."

I left the men to their work, and in a few minutes I was back on the sunny trail with the cool breeze riffling in my face.

* * *

I made my camp that evening in a place where a spring came out of the side of the mountain. On the other side of the spring, some fifty yards back in the timber, sat two cabins. One of them was clearly past all use, as its roof had fallen in and the front door was missing. The other one, the larger of the two cabins, looked as if it was abandoned but might be liveable. The windows were boarded up, and a rusty padlock hung on the front door. It had a gable roof, covered over with rusty sheet metal but still holding together. On the front and back, poles jutted out from the roof ridge and from each end of the eaves. I imagined those poles would be handy for hanging things like ham or bacon, or maybe a deer carcass, out of the reach of bears. I didn't like to think unkindly thoughts, but the stout ridge pole looked as if it would do to hang a horse thief as well. I wondered what the inside of the cabin was like, but with everything shut up and no good reason for me to go snooping, I rolled out my blankets on the ground and left the cabin to itself with its dark contents.

On the other side of the mountains I came out onto the rolling plains, good grassland paling in the late summer sun. With every mile the elevation dropped a little until I came to the town of Seneca on the North Platte River. As I understood the layout, Rawlins lay north and west, while the sheep camp where Fernando was to have gone lay almost due west. Although I didn't know whether he had come this way, I thought it pretty likely that he did. So I saw this town as a kind of jumping-off place, and I decided I would try to do a thorough job of asking questions here.

The town itself gave me a comfortable feeling. After crossing the pass where mountains of rock were capped with permanent snowfields and where juniper trees had been tortured and twisted by winds whipping across the open flats, I was struck by the tidiness of painted houses, flower beds, plots of lawn, and half-grown shade trees that looked as if they stood a good chance of making it to full growth. Seneca didn't have the hard-bitten look of a railroad town or the pinched look of a town along a freight trail. People had come here to live.

In the first place I stopped, a general store, I learned that the town had some mineral springs—not as many or as big as in Warm Springs or Thermopolis, but enough to attract a few visitors. Out of that I concluded that some people came here to die, but even at that the town seemed like a place for the living.

When I asked the proprietor if he had seen someone of Fernando's description, he shook his head and said he didn't keep a close eye on who came and went, but I might have better luck in a place called the White Owl. The fellas in there didn't miss much, he said.

I found the White Owl down the street a couple of blocks. It sat on my right, on the east side of the main street, where the slanting sunlight of late afternoon glared on the picture window. I tied my horse to the hitching rail in front of the window, where I could keep an eye on him, and I went in.

I expected to hear a bell on the door, for as I first

looked through the glass I took the place to be a tobacconist's. Once inside, though, I saw that it was also a place where men gathered for drinks and conversation. Unlike so many dark saloons I had known, the interior of this one was well lit and more or less in the public eye. Given the nature of the place, it didn't need a bell on the door.

Along the wall on my left sat the counter, with shelves behind it, which I had seen through the glass on the door. Although I don't smoke or chew, I appreciated the full supply of cigars, smoking tobacco, and chewing tobacco. In the glass case beneath the counter I saw a selection of briar, stone, and clay pipes that made me think of my friend Tome. At the far end of the counter, mounted on what looked like a podium of honor, perched the namesake of the establishment. Some taxidermist had done a good job with him, and he looked as if he got dusted off from time to time, for he was clean and dignified.

Against the opposite wall ran a dark wooden bar, with a small mirror in back of it. The spittoons and the brass rail were clean, and no one stood at the bar on either side. In the middle of the room, the two tables closest to the front window were unoccupied, as were the tables toward the back. At the other five tables, sitting in groups of two, three, and four, men sat with drinks in front of them. A haze of smoke hung in the air, and I had not disturbed the hum of conversation when I came in.

I crossed the room with two empty tables on my left. As I looked down the bar, a man rose from where he had been sitting on a stool and reading a newspaper in the light that came in through the window. I took him in at a glance, a man about forty with his thinning hair well combed, a clean-shaven man in a white shirt and dark tie. He moved to the middle of the bar, where I met him and ordered a beer.

As he poured my drink, something on the wall caught my attention. Looking up, I saw that it was a piece of art work framed in dark wood and measuring a foot and a half wide by two feet tall. It showed the profile of an Indian head with one feather sticking up, the whole outline punched out of a sheet of copper with neatly spaced small-caliber bullet holes. I had seen this style of art before, with horse heads and ducks and such, and I admired the kind of precision a shooter would have to have. This one seemed to fit in just right with the tone of the place.

The bartender served me my beer and stood with his back to the mirror. Off to his right side I could see the reflection of the White Owl on his perch across the room.

"Nice day," said the bartender.

"Sure is." I sipped my beer. I gathered that this was a place where a fellow paid when he was done, not each time he got served.

"Passin' through?"

"That I am."

"Good weather for it."

"Yes, it is." I took another drink of beer. "Quite a few people come through this way, I imagine."

"Oh, indeed."

"I don't suppose anyone bothers to remember 'em from one day to the next."

"Maybe some." The man was looking at his right hand, where he rubbed his fingertips with his thumb. Then he looked up as if to say he didn't mind if I asked.

"I'm followin' up on a friend of mine who might have come through here about a month ago, maybe a little more."

"By himself?"

"I think so. He would have been a Mexican fellow. Clean, well-dressed, a little taller than average."

The bartender twisted his mouth and frowned. "Don't know. I don't remember anyone by that description coming in here. But that doesn't mean he didn't come through town." He looked over at one of the tables. "We could ask Henry. He sees as much as anyone does." The bartender stepped forward and raised his voice just a little as he called Henry's name.

A man in a brown wool vest and white shirt sleeves looked up, and at the bartender's beckoning he came and stood next to me. He was a short man, soft around the middle and going gray where he still had hair.

"What is it, Mick?"

"This man is trying to find a friend of his who might have come through here. I told him you know everything that goes on in this town, upstairs and down, day and night."

"I wish I did. It would be worth something." The man turned to me, his brown eyes scanning me. "What kind of man is he, this friend you're looking for?"

"A decent sort," I said. "Mexican fellow, taller than you or me. Clean-looking, usually goes well dressed. Might have had a bundle with him."

Henry's eyebrows went up, and he pursed his lips. "Oh, I might have seen someone like that."

"Really?"

"How long ago would it have been?"

"About a month, maybe a little more."

"I think it could have been him. You say he had a bundle."

"I'm pretty sure he would have."

Henry nodded. "A fellow like that stayed at my hotel." He motioned with his head toward the street. "I've got the Twin Star Hotel—which you're welcome to stop at, of course."

I tipped my head in agreement.

"I remember him because, like you said, he was a little cleaner than most of 'em, and he had this package. He handled it with a lot of care."

"It would have been a figurine of the Virgin. He was taking it to some other fellows out on a ranch."

"I remember him, all right. Looked like the kind that might be carryin' a little money."

"Probably no more than he needed. But he likes to look good wherever he goes. You don't remember which way he was going when he left here, do you?"

"No, not at all. I just remember the bundle, and his shiny boots."

"Well, thanks a lot. I appreciate it."

"Don't mention it. I hope you find him." His eyes traveled over me again. "You say he's a friend of yours, and not just someone you're lookin' for?"

"Well, yes, he's a kind of a friend. More like a friend of some people who are good friends of mine, if you follow me."

"Uh-huh." He took a cigar out of his vest pocket and held it without biting off the end or lighting it.

"And they're the ones who worried when he

didn't come back. They asked me to come see what I could find out."

"Sure. Then you're not some kind of a bounty hunter—not that I'd object, you understand." He waved the cigar at me. "There's men that ought to be caught."

It seemed as if he was willing to believe that the well-dressed Mexican was some kind of a criminal, but I didn't think he would be disappointed with the truth. "No, I'm not. Just on an errand for some friends."

"Well, like I say, feel welcome to stop at the Twin Star. I think you'll find it decent enough."

"Thank you." I shook his hand, and he went back to his table. I didn't watch him long enough to see if he lit his cigar.

The bartender, who had stood by and listened, now had a satisfied look on his face. "If anyone knows, Henry does."

"Seems like it." Then a stray image crossed my mind. "Huh. I wished I'd thought to ask him about this other thing."

"What's that?"

"If he knows a fellow named Milaham."

The bartender's eyebrows tightened. "Who, now?"

"A man named Milaham. Some sort of a hunter of lost people. Do you know him? He's got one bad eye, and you're never sure if he's lookin' at you."

The bartender nodded. "I know of him. They say he can roll dice and watch the chicken fights at the same time."

"He comes through here, then?"

"Oh, yeh."

I motioned with my head toward the tables. "Does he stay at Henry's hotel?"

"I wouldn't think so."

By the time I drank two beers in the White Owl, the shadows were stretching out to the middle of the street. I figured this town was as good a place as any to put up for the night, and I imagined the Twin Star might even have a bathtub.

I found the sign right away—large red letters on a white background. The other two hotels on the main street, the Plains and the Lincoln, had smaller signs with black lettering. The Twin Star also had a railed veranda, but I imagined the red lettering would have been more eye-catching to Fernando. I stopped the horse in front of the hotel, swung down, and tied him at the rack.

As I walked up the steps of the Twin Star, I noticed they were worn and I felt them give as they creaked. The horseshoe above the front door had gone rusty long ago, and the veranda sagged at one corner. I thought Henry sized me up pretty well. His hotel was none too rich for my blood, and I imagined Fernando had seen it the same way.

CHAPTER FOUR

A man who was younger than Henry but even softer around the middle signed me into a room. I told him I had met Henry earlier in the day and had talked with him about a traveler who had spent the night about a month earlier.

After I described Fernando, the man nodded and said, "Oh, yes. I remember him. He didn't say much. Just the bare phrases to get by."

He slid the key across the counter to me, and as I picked it up, Henry appeared at my right.

"Well, hello. Glad to see you chose to stay here."

"Seemed like the best place."

"We think so." He gave an automatic smile. "You might be happy to know that the Twin Star has a dining room. For the overnight guests and the regular lodgers both."

"That sounds fine."

He smiled again. "Supper should be served in about an hour and a half."

"What are the chances of getting a bath?"

"Oh, the best time for a bath would be a little while after supper. Unless you want a cold bath," he added with a heh-heh.

"Not if I can get a hot one."

"We'll make sure you do."

I carried my personal things up to the room, then went downstairs to put my horse in a stable. After that I went back to see about relaxing in the room, and I still had an hour. I stretched out on the bed, which sank in the middle, so I sat up on the side and looked around. The room was a narrow little affair, with the bed taking up half the space. Other than that, there was a spindly wooden chair, a washstand with no basin or pitcher, and a dresser. I tried the drawers and had to pull them out in crooked jerks. Three hooks on the wall served to hang clothes, and the rug on the floor would have to be rotated ninety degrees for anyone with feet larger than average. The room lay on the back or west side of the building, on the second floor, so it was warm and stuffy in the later afternoon. The window seemed to have been painted shut, so I gave up on trying to get the place ventilated. I decided to go downstairs and sit on the veranda until suppertime.

I hadn't been sitting there very long when a polite-looking man came up the steps. He wore a gray, lightweight wool suit and vest with a white shirt and black tie. He looked at me as if he intended to talk to me, and I wasn't surprised when he reached the deck of the veranda and came my way.

"Good afternoon," he said as he drew nearer.

"Good afternoon."

"Do you mind if I sit here?"

"Not at all." I tipped my head toward the chair on my left.

I saw now that he was very tidy and trim. He had well-groomed dark hair that was turning gray, and he was clean-shaven. For all his restraint he had an anxious air about him, and his slender build might well have come from worry as much as from good eating habits.

"Are you traveling?" he asked.

"Yes, I am."

"Not bad weather for it."

"No, it isn't."

"I hope you don't think I'm being too forward, sitting down like this."

"Not at all. After a few days on my own, I don't mind the company."

He waited a long moment until he spoke again. "Which way might you be headed, if you don't mind?"

I shrugged. "I'm not sure yet. I think I'll go west, but I may go around to the north."

"Oh, yes. I see. Again, if you don't mind, I understand you're looking for someone."

My glance met his. He had serious, dark eyes, and I could not see a particle of guile in him. "Yes, I am. Did Henry tell you that?"

"No, I heard it less directly. The people who work for him talk across the alley to a person who works for me." He gave me an earnest look. "I'm a dentist, you see. Alfred McCabe."

He hesitated, as if he didn't want to thrust his hand at me. When I reached over to shake, his hand came forward. He had a strong grip, which I suppose is good in a dentist. When he rested both hands in his lap, I noticed they were slender.

"My name's Jimmy Clevis," I said. "I'm looking

for a fellow named Fernando." At that moment I remembered something Chanate had told me, something I hadn't had the occasion to think of. "His last name is Molina Valdés, with an *s*."

Dr. McCabe nodded.

"He's a friend of some friends of mine, down in Colorado. He came up this way, apparently passed through this town, but did not make it to the place where he was headed."

"I see."

"Henry says he stayed here, but no one, including the help, seems to remember very much about him. You don't happen to remember anything, do you?"

He shook his head. "No, I'm afraid I don't. But I hope you find him."

"So do I."

Dr. McCabe was quiet for another minute, and then he said, "You're probably wondering why I took it upon myself to sit down here, if it wasn't to say something that might help you find your friend."

"The thought might occur to me."

"Well, Mr. Clevis, to put it directly, I'm looking for someone, too."

I tried to see in him something I hadn't seen yet, but I couldn't make out anything more than a man who worked hard at watching how he said things.

He must have read my uncertainty. "I don't mean to say I'm going out on a search myself. I tried it for a while, but I had to give it up. It was consuming me. And after all, I have a practice here to look after."

"Of course."

He took a calm, measured breath. "What I mean, Mr. Clevis, is that I have lost somebody, and I am hoping someone can find her."

"I see." I figured he must be the doctor I heard about in Laramie.

After a deep breath, he went on. "My daughter. She disappeared a little over eight years ago, and our life has gone to pieces. As I said, I went out many times and scoured every place she might have gone on foot, and finally we accepted the idea that she must have been carried away. It has worried me sick, and it has ruined my wife's health. Mary was our only child."

"I'm sorry to hear this, Doctor."

"Thank you. Everyone says that, of course, but not everyone really means it. You seem to, and I don't feel so bad for making you listen to me."

"I don't mind at all, I assure you."

"Well, thanks." He took another full breath. "And so, even after the time that has gone by, we still hold onto the hope that she might turn up somewhere."

"You've tried other ways to find her?"

"Oh, yes. After my own futile attempts I hired an investigator, who probably did an honest job but came back with nothing. Since then I've contracted with a couple of other men to keep an eye out for anything that might lead us to her."

"Is one of them named Milaham?"

"Yes, Ross Milaham. Do you know him?"

"I've met him in passing."

"I don't know how good he is, but he seems to travel a wide circuit. Whenever he comes through this way, I hear from him, but I don't know how much he really does."

"I barely know him," I said.

"Of course." The doctor hesitated, looked at his hands, and then held me steady with his eyes.

"What I'd like to ask you, Mr. Clevis, is whether you might keep an eye out for me as well."

I shrugged. "I can certainly make note of anything I happen to see, but I don't think I can look for two people at once. It's not my regular line of work, and I'm mainly on an errand for some friends."

"I understand. But if some bit of information, or some impression, were to come your way—"

"I'd be sure to pass it on."

"I would be willing to make it worth your while if you did find—"

I held up my hand. "If I learn anything, I'll share it with you as a matter of good will." I did not want to tell him that I would rather avoid any sense of obligation, and I think he understood. I was sure he had had many conversations like this one, and I was sure he had been given the brush-off in several of them, for he seemed willing to accept whatever the other person would agree to.

"I appreciate your goodness of heart," he said.

"It's all right." As the uneasiness seemed to have leveled off, I ventured a step further. "If you had a picture of her, or a description, I'd have a better idea of what I was on the lookout for."

He gave a short nod, reached inside his coat, and drew out a photograph. After he handed it to me, I tipped it to try to catch better light. The photo was bent and worn, as well it might be from eight years of being taken out and shown, but I could see the girl's face well enough. She was a plain-looking girl, dark-haired and big-toothed.

"How old is she in this picture?"

"Nine years old." Then he added, "She was wearing this same necklace when she disappeared."

I strained to see the little specks. "Are those diamonds?"

"Not real ones. Just something for a young girl. But the garnet is real. It had been my mother's."

I made out a larger jewel that hung like a pendant. "I see." I stared at the photograph for another minute and then handed it back to him. I imagined some version of the same picture had been in the sheaf I saw Milaham flip through.

"I appreciate any word you might have," said the doctor as he tucked the photograph back inside his jacket. "And if there's anything I can do for you, I'll be glad to."

"Good enough." I stood up as he did, and I felt his strong grip again as we shook hands. "It's been a pleasure meeting you, Dr. McCabe."

"Likewise. I wish you all the best."

As he walked away, I was struck again with a sense of how well he mastered his own desperation.

Things took on a cheerier note at suppertime. The meal itself consisted of beefsteak and fried potatoes, which I never disagree with. Three of the regular lodgers bolted their food and got up, but the other two sat around for a few minutes after the meal and talked about how good the local fishing was. Then they withdrew and left the table to me and another traveler whose name I understood to be Grimes.

My first impression of this fellow was that he had a very fitting name. In addition to wearing a gray wool overshirt that had dirt and grease worn into the very grain of it, he had large, rough hands, smudged and calloused. His fingernails were ragged, and the few that were not broken or chipped had quarter-moons of black dirt that a tidier man would have scraped out with a knife. His face was blemished to the point that I wouldn't know what could be washed off and what couldn't. He had large, wide eyes, a full nose, and a dark bushy beard. From the beginning he was a friendly, outgoing sort, and whenever he laughed he showed a remarkable mouth. His teeth, those that he still had, bore a yellow, cheesy texture that made a contrast with the dark gaps here and there. He was also missing half of his left index finger, but the round nub seemed to work fine when he rolled a cigarette. I watched him roll a couple of them, and he was pretty handy at it.

When we had the table to ourselves, he turned to me and smiled. "What's yer line, partner?"

"Oh, I'm a workin' man."

"So am I. I'm a teamster."

Axle grease, I thought. "I suppose that's a good line of work."

He laughed. "Sometimes. When you're not sloggin' in the mud or wrestlin' with mules." He blew a double stream of smoke out through his nostrils. "Cowpuncher?"

"I've done some of that, and I like it as well as anything. Right now I'm just on an errand. Doing some work for some friends."

"Work's work." He laughed again. "And none of it pays enough. Isn't that the truth?"

"Sure is."

"I'll tell ya, if I had a nickel for every night I had to

sleep under the wagon in the rain, tryin' to remember what it's like to be inside a warm, dry place—say, you ever been down by Nueva Cassa Grand?"

"Um, no."

"They've got some places there. A girl showed me a trick with a knotted scarf that I won't forget."

"I've heard of that."

"Yeh, it's somethin'. So where's yer errand takin' you?"

"I'm not sure yet."

"How's that?"

"Well, I'm lookin' for a fellow who came through this way and never showed up where he was supposed to go. They say he stopped here—stayed in this same hotel, in fact—but I don't know if he went west from here or if he went north and around."

"By Rawlins."

"That's right. And I don't know exactly how things are laid out going west of here."

He shrugged. "It ain't much. About a day's ride from this place there's a town called Raven Springs. After that, there's more rangeland, some of it poorer than what you see around here. Some of it damn poor."

"He was headed for a sheep camp out that way."

"There's sheep there, that's for sure." Grimes brushed at his beard. "What kind of a fellow did you say he was?"

"I don't know if I did, but he's a little taller than average, usually goes well dressed. Mexican. Doesn't talk much, especially in English."

"Huh. What'd he do to get folks lookin' for him?"

"Nothin', that I know of. He's a friend of some

people I know. He was supposed to visit this sheep camp, and no one ever heard from him."

"Ain't that somethin'?" Grimes tipped his ash in his hand and rubbed it on his trouser leg. "Was he carryin' money?"

"Not much, I wouldn't think. The one thing that might have had some value was that he was carryin' one of those religious figurines."

"Oh, yeh. They're crazy about that stuff."

"Uh-huh."

"So he just disappeared? And he didn't have anything valuable enough to run off with?"

I shook my head. "Not that I know of."

"And not enough for someone to want to do somethin' to him?"

"I don't think so."

"Huh." He looked at the stub of his cigarette, which he had smoked down to where there couldn't be but a grain or two of tobacco left. He pinched the lit end, rubbed it between his thumb and forefinger, and dropped it on the floor. "World must be full of missin' people."

"That's what you'd think. Have you met the dentist here?"

Grimes shook his head. "No, but I've heard of him. Sort of a sad case. Lost his little girl, I guess."

"I felt sorry for him, myself."

"Uh-huh. I'll tell ya, if I was you I'd go to Raven Springs."

"Is that right?"

He just nodded.

"Have you been there?"

"Long time ago."

"What makes you think that's where I ought to go?"

"I think it might be one of the last places that missing people go through."

"Really?"

"What's yer missin' pal's name?"

"Fernando," I said, knocking the Spanish edges off the word. "Fernando Molina Valdés."

"That's one." He dug the makings out of the pocket of his wool overshirt. "And I might know of another."

I waited as he made slick work out of rolling another cigarette and lighting it. I could tell he liked being someone who might know something, so I let him proceed at his own pace.

He shook out the match and dropped it on the floor. "What did you say yer name is?"

"I don't know that I did, but it's Jimmy. Jimmy Clevis."

"Well, I'll give you my full name, so we know each other. It's Benjamin Grimes. Ben to most people."

"Good enough." I shook his hand.

"So here's what I think," he said. "You're looking for a man that disappeared somewhere out here. I'm lookin' for another, for a fella named Milt Lawhorn, and I think he might've ended up in the same place. Put two 'n' two together, Jimmy."

It was my turn to nod. "Is this fellow Lawhorn a friend of yours?"

"He's my partner. Or might be he *was* my partner. I don't know. But he was supposed to come out this way, lookin' for mules to buy. The last time anyone saw him was here in Seneca, just like yore man. I been up and down the line to Rawlins and back, and no one's seen him past this point. That tells me he probably went west."

"That sounds reasonable. Say, do you know a man named Milaham?"

"You mean Miller. Wolf Miller. Mule skinner."

"No, I mean Milaham. Ross Milaham. He makes a livin' out of lookin' for lost people."

"Well, I don't, then. What about him?"

"I was just wonderin' if you'd talked to him about your friend."

"Nah, what do I want to pay someone else for, to do somethin' I can do myself?"

"My friends chose not to pay him, either. I just wondered if you know him."

"Not at all."

"No harm in that."

"I'd say not."

"It's probably good to know about him, though, in case your paths cross."

"You know him, then?"

"I've met him."

"Is he on the square?"

"I don't know."

"Well, to hell with him. But I'll tell you what, Jimmy. Maybe you and me can do somethin'." He held his cigarette out in front of his mouth and looked at me with one eye wider than the other.

"Like what?"

"Here's an idea. What say you and me both go to Raven Springs, but not together?"

"Discreet-like?"

"That's it. You go first, you let on like you're on some kind of business, and then I'll show up later. Make like we don't know each other. That way, one of us might find out somethin' the other one don't."

"Not a bad idea. And we can kind of keep an eye on one another."

He gave a short laugh, showing the wreckage of his mouth. "I can take care of myself, as far as that goes."

"I didn't mean it any other way, and as far as that's concerned, if we had to look out for one another, we'd probably be better off together."

"Might be." He flicked his ash in front of him and rubbed it into his lap. "I've just got a hunch we'll find somethin' there."

Before the conversation went any further, an older, heavyset woman came into the room. I had seen her sweeping the hallway earlier, and I took her to be the housekeeper. She paused at the end of the table and then told me I could have a bath now if I wanted it.

I stood up and looked at Grimes. "If I don't see you later this evening, then I'll see you at breakfast."

He smiled, showing less of his mouth than before. "You bet, Jimmy."

I followed the stout woman down the hallway, and when she stopped at a doorway, I stopped as well. "Excuse me," I said, "but do you remember the Mexican gentleman who stayed here about a month ago?" I figured she had already heard what I was looking for.

"Just a little," she said.

"I don't suppose he mentioned where he planned to go the next day."

"No, he didn't talk much."

"I didn't think he would. Did he take a bath, though?"

"Oh, yes, he did. Right in this same place. He was so clean, and taller than most, that you wouldn't know he was Mexican until he said something." She pushed the door open. "The towel's on the chair. Soap's in the little dish. The door locks from the inside, right here."

Once inside, I locked the door and got undressed, then let myself down into the warm bath. Now that I was on Fernando's trail, it seemed strange to be staying in the same hotel and bathing in the same tub. I felt vulnerable, and even though I had no fear that someone would come in to stab or shoot me in the bathtub, I was glad I had the door locked.

The next morning at breakfast, Grimes was as cheerful as before and no cleaner. I knew it was none of my business, but I wished he had taken advantage of some of the soap and hot water in the Twin Star. As for whatever else the town had to offer, I guessed he had found some of that. His eyes looked bleary, and I thought his hand wavered as he spooned himself some fried potatoes. Otherwise he gave no indication of feeling worse for the wear.

"Sleep all right?" he asked.

"Like a baby. And yourself?"

"Never a problem."

After we had each eaten a few mouthfuls, I said, "Are you still in the deal on what we talked about last night?"

"Oh, yeh." He took a drink of coffee. "No change. You go first, and I'll come moseyin' in later. The town's not so big that we can't find each other."

"That's fine. I don't think I'll state my real business at all."

He looked at me across the top of his coffee cup. "Me neither." He took another swallow, then said,

"Between the two of us, we ought to be able to turn up somethin'."

He didn't seem inclined to talk any more, so I left it at that and ate in silence. I noticed that he chewed with some difficulty, stretching his jaw and shifting his food. I imagined a dentist had pulled at least some of the teeth he was missing, and I thought again that a pair of strong hands must be a very good asset to a man like Dr. McCabe, especially when he had to yank against something as indestructible as a man like Grimes.

CHAPTER FIVE

The little dark horse and I didn't waste any time, leaving right after breakfast and keeping up a good pace. The weather was comfortable but not too warm, and the rolling plains country made for easy traveling. The wide open stretches took some getting used to, with a distant hill always farther than I thought at first, but as I rode through the day and took it in at its own rate, the country began to make sense to me. The prairie dogs and the antelope watched me pass through, and the sun overhead made its slow steady course until I had to tip my hat brim to it. In the middle of the afternoon I topped a rise and saw the first clump of trees I had seen since morning. In another twenty minutes I came to the outskirts of Raven Springs.

I had been prepared to think of this town as a place that swallowed up travelers, so I studied it as I rode up to the first pair of establishments. They looked like two inns or roadhouses, one on each side of the trail, and my first impression was that they served as a portal or entryway. Then it occurred to me that the town proper had been settled first, and then some latecomers had built these roadside inns to catch travelers before they got to the town itself.

They were both wooden structures, no doubt built by different parties. The two-story place on the left, according to a short plank with letters burned into it, was the Empire Inn. The sign board, which was nailed above the front door and protected by the overhang of the porch, looked a little newer than the rest of the building. Either the carpenters had been stingy with the nails or the original lumber had been very green, for the exterior boards were gray, weathered, and warped.

Across the road, the single-storied Falconer House had a sturdier look to it. The inn was built in the style of a mountain lodge, framed with heavy timbers supporting a high gabled roof. The building had a broad front porch with a log railing, and between the top and second rails was fastened a plank twice as wide and long as the neighbor's. The name of the establishment had been engraved in the plank and then filled with a black substance, probably tar but maybe some other kind of caulking that had been painted, for the letters had a shine.

I tried to imagine how Fernando might have seen these two places. My inner sense told me he would have gone to the one that looked less expensive, so I tied my horse in front of the Empire Inn and stepped up onto the board porch. The main entry door was open, and through the screen I could hear a human voice and the soft clatter that would come from kitchen work.

Inside, I found the hotel desk in a small front room where wallpaper had begun to lift along the seams. Four wooden armchairs faced the middle of the room, and I could imagine them in cold weather being turned toward the wood stove in the corner. I stood halfway between the entryway and desk until a man came out from the inner quarters.

"Afternoon," he said, taking his place behind the counter as I stepped forward. "How can I help you today?"

"Lookin' for a place to stay." As I spoke, I took as full a glance of him as I could without staring.

He was about forty years old, starting to grow heavy in his features. He bore a broad resemblance to various men I had known from Texas and Oklahoma, men whose parents might have come during the potato famine. He had sandy hair, a rough complexion, side levers and a mustache that joined them, and a few days' stubble on his chin and lower jowls.

His flat blue eyes seemed to be giving me a looking-over. "Just fine," he said. "One night, or more?"

"Maybe more, depending on how my work goes."

"Ohhh." He raised his chin. "I think you should find our inn quite satisfactory."

I looked around at the empty chairs. "Looks fine to me."

He opened a ledger, where all the names seemed to be written in the same hand. "Name, sir?"

"Um, I'd like to be sure of the price, first."

"Oh, of course. Dollar a day. That includes everything—meals, stable, bath once a week. More if you absolutely need it, dependin' on your work."

I didn't speak for a moment, as if I was considering it.

"Sound agreeable?"

"Sure," I said. I took out a silver dollar and laid it on the counter. I could see his eyes go right to it. "Let's try one night, and I'll know by tomorrow whether I need to stay longer."

"Just fine," he said with a business-like nod. "Name, then?" He dipped a pen in a bottle of ink that already stood opened.

I figured the fewer the falsehoods, the better, and I hadn't agreed on anything different with Ben Grimes. "Clevis," I said. "Jimmy Clevis."

He started writing. "Coming from?"

"Laramie, for the present."

"Good enough." He dipped his pen a second time and scratched across the page.

I must have let my mind go absent as I watched him scrawl my information, for all of a sudden I was aware that another person stood at his left elbow. The first thing I saw was a pair of beady dark eyes, then a face surrounded by a head scarf knotted below the chin and met by a high collar. A little bit of drab brown hair was showing, and a dull sheen of sweat glistened on the cheekbones. I caught the smell of kitchen grease, which, along with the apron that covered the stout body, gave me the idea that this was the cook.

The innkeeper turned and said, not very loud, "This is Mr. Clevis. He'll be staying at least one night." Then he faced me and held his arm up over the counter. "I'm Cale Gridley."

"Pleased to meet you." I shook his hand.

"And this is Norma. Mrs. Gridley."

"How do you do?" I said, working up a smile as I met the expressionless face.

Norma's lips barely moved. "Hello."

Mr. Gridley's voice came out louder now, as if to compensate for Norma's muffled speech. "Why don't you sit down, Mr. Clevis, and rest a little. It'll take the girl a few minutes to get your room ready." He turned to Norma and said, "Go ahead and tell Penny."

Norma didn't move right away, but as I turned to look at the chairs on my left, I saw movement from the corner of my eye. When I faced Mr. Gridley again, he was alone.

"Have a seat, Mr. Clevis."

"Just call me Jimmy," I said.

"Call me Cale if you want. It's short for Caleb, but nobody's ever called me that but preachers and judges." He smiled with his mouth closed.

I took a seat and tried to look relaxed. "This is a nice location you've got."

"Oh, it'll do. Sometimes we wish for a little more business."

"Isn't that always the case, though? Seems like no matter how much you make, you could do with a little more to come out even."

"Oh, yeh." He had taken out a toothpick from somewhere and was working on his teeth. "Long ride from Laramie," he said.

"It's not so bad. And the weather's been fine."

"Couldn't wish for any better."

I had the impression that he was stalling around for something, but I didn't know what. I was already convinced that he and Norma were capable of plucking any traveler as clean as a Christmas goose, but I didn't think he would make a move quite this soon. To do my own form of stalling, I took out my pocketknife and started cleaning my fingernails.

The door from the inner quarters moved, catching

my eye, and a woman I had not seen before came into the reception area and stood by the end of the counter. As she said something in a low voice to Mr. Gridley, I wondered if this was the person he had referred to as Penny.

I looked at her, and she smiled with her mouth closed. I thought she was a little old for someone to be referring to her as a girl, but I didn't know Mr. Gridley or his speech habits well enough to guess.

Then he spoke up. "Jimmy, this is my sister, Jeanette. She helps us out here. Jeanette, this is Jimmy."

She crossed in front of the counter, holding her hands together in front of her, then turned to face me from ten feet away. I could see the resemblance now. Her hair was lighter than his but had a similar texture, and her eyes had the same blue tone. She couldn't have been but a few years behind him in age, as her face had begun to sag. She wore a loose-fitting charcoal-colored dress, and beneath it her body looked as if it had begun to sag as well.

"Won't you sit down?" I said, motioning with my hand toward a chair.

"Thank you." She smoothed the bottom of her dress as she took a seat. "I came to tell Cale that your room will be a few more minutes yet."

"No hurry," I said. "I'm just relaxin' after a day's travel."

She smiled again, this time showing where one front tooth was missing. "I've been workin' all day, too," she said, "and I don't mind getting off my feet for a few minutes."

"Jimmy's from Laramie," said her brother.

"Oh, is that right? What brings you here?"

I could see her eyes better now, a flat blue that reminded me of a lifeless winter sky. "I'm on a business venture," I answered.

"Oh?" She moved in her hair.

"Yes. I'm on my way to the Red Desert, to look for stray horses."

Gridley's voice came up. "That's quite a little ways yet."

"Uh-huh."

Jeanette smiled again in her close-mouthed way that made her face wrinkle around her mouth. "Is this some work you're doin' for somebody else?"

"That's right. There's a fellow in Laramie who's puttin' up for the expenses and all, and it's up to me to find the horses. I've got a little pamphlet with a description of the horses, the brands, and such."

"That's a big country," said Gridley, still working the toothpick in his teeth.

"So I understand. I expect I might be out there for a while."

"What makes you think you might want to spend more than one night here? Do you think there's stray horses here?"

"Oh, no. It's just that I'm startin' to wonder if I don't need a second horse. We came a long ways today, from ten miles the other side of Seneca, and I'm wonderin' if that little horse might play out on me."

"He looks like he's in good shape to me."

"I thought he was. He came over the mountains plumb fine, but he sulled on me a couple of times today."

"Hah. Maybe you're pushin' him too hard and you need to feed him better. We'll make sure he eats good tonight."

I smiled at him. "I appreciate that."

He took the toothpick out of his mouth. "Well, then, how much do you think you might have to pay for a horse around here?"

"Well, that's just it. I hope I don't have to. This fella that's stakin' me is kinda tight. He give me just enough to get by on."

"Oh, so you're not exactly in business for yourself."

"Only insofar as I stand to make so much a head for anything I can round up."

"If they're on your list."

"Sure."

"Then this fellow in Laramie is more like your boss."

"You could say that."

"Huh." He went back to picking his teeth.

"It's not so bad, though," I said. "I don't let very much bother me. The last fella that worked for him got mad and quit because the boss sent someone out to check on him. I figure if you're not up to anything, what have you got to worry about?" I looked at Jeanette. "Don't you think?"

She bobbed her head up and down.

"That's the best way," said her brother.

"You ever hear of Black Ned?" I asked, trying to think of small talk.

"Oh, yeh. They put a bullet through him. That's what I heard."

"Pulled too many fast ones." I directed my gaze at Jeanette, who gave me an earnest look in return. Then I spoke to Mr. Gridley. "What I hope is, I get on that horse in the mornin' and he's sound as a dollar, and I rowel on out of here."

"And on to the Red Desert," said Jeanette.

"That's right. Where was Black Ned from, by the way?"

Mr. Gridley answered. "He worked this whole country, from Brown's Park over to Rattlesnake Pass, but originally he came up from Texas, I believe."

"Didn't he have any friends?"

"Yeh, but it didn't do him any good. One of them got it too, at about the same time."

"Were you here when they strung up Big Nose?"

Gridley shook his head. "Nah. That was before we came here."

"Oh, then you didn't build this place."

"No, it was already here."

I caught a glance at Jeanette, who didn't seem troubled by any of this talk. I thought she might be a pretty hard woman, just from the looks of her.

At that moment, the door from the back quarters opened again, and a girl about fifteen years old came into the room. She had hair the color of dark straw, and for a moment I thought she might have been a daughter to either the older man or his sister, except that she kept her head down in the submissive way of a servant girl. She said something in a low voice, then raised her head and looked at me. She had large brown eyes, and her facial features were narrower than those of Gridley or Jeanette.

The innkeeper spoke up. "Penny says your room is ready." He held up a skeleton key with a leather tag attached to the head. "Room Six. We've got you on the ground floor here, through the dining room and down the hall." He waved with his left hand and then set the key on the counter.

When the girl turned and left, I saw that the door she went through was not only silent but also swung both ways. I figured that was how Norma had come and gone so quiet-like.

I turned to Jeanette and said, "Looks like you've got the whole family here."

"Oh, that's not anyone in the family," she said. "That's a little orphan girl they took in, her and her brother. But we're all just like a family."

"That's nice," I offered. "Not everybody gets a chance like that." Nobody spoke for a few seconds, so I stood up and said, "Well, what do you think if I put my horse away first? I don't have much to bring in, and I can fetch it from the stable."

"Sure," said Mr. Gridley. He picked up the key. "Go ahead and take this now, and come and go as you wish."

"I see. I don't need to check the key in when I go out?"

He smiled. "This isn't the city. But you already knew that."

I took the key. "Go around this side for the stable?"

"Around the south side, uh-huh. That's easiest. The stable's right in back. Tim should be there."

I went out into the warm afternoon, where Negrito stood dozing at the hitch rack. I patted him on the neck as I untied the reins, and then I led him around the building. I found the stable in back all right, but as I turned the corner I almost walked on top of a boy who was holding a dog down onto the ground. He was a light-haired boy, the kind I've heard some people call a sunhead, and the dog looked like a mongrel.

"Well, hello there," I said, stopping short.

He looked up and around at me with pale blue eyes and a blank expression on his face. He didn't say anything.

"What's your name, fella?"

"Ollie." He didn't look straight at me when he answered.

"That's a good name. Do you like dogs?"

"I guess."

"Are you Penny's little brother?"

"I guess."

"How old are you?" I knew that all little kids had a definite answer to that question.

"Nine."

"Well, I'll tell you what. I'm stayin' here at the inn tonight, and I'm puttin' my horse away right now. Is there a man named Tim somewhere around?"

At that moment I heard the creak of hinges, and the stable door opened. A man stood in the doorway, squinting at me.

"Hello," I called as I walked toward him. "I'm puttin' up at the inn this evening, and Mr. Gridley told me to look for Tim."

"That's me. Bring 'im in."

The stable man stood back just enough for me to lead the horse past him. He was a lean, stoop-shouldered man in a canvas overall, and I got a close-up look at his face as I walked right in front of it. He had a narrow chin and small eyes, the left one closer to center, so it looked as if he was keeping an eye on his nose. He wore an old battered hat clamped down on a thatch of hair that looked like last year's meadow hay. He followed me into the stable and pulled the door halfway shut.

"That stall right there," he said, and I noticed he had picked up a cane to point with.

I stripped the gear from the horse and hung it on a rack, then untied my duffel bag from the saddle.

With my side out of the stable man's view, I dug into my pocket and felt for a two-bit piece.

"My name's Jimmy Clevis," I said as I pressed it into his palm. "I'm staying in Room Six."

"Tim Holman. I keep a good eye on things."

"I'm sure you do." I smiled and walked out into the sunlight, where Ollie still had the dog pinned to the ground. He gave me a blank stare as I walked by, but neither of us said anything.

As I went back around to the hotel entrance, I paused before I walked out in front of the overhang. Past the other end of the porch, I saw something that held me for a minute. Jeanette had Penny by the elbow and was walking her across the road to the Falconer House. I waited until they went in before I stepped into view, walked around the porch, and on up into the hotel.

I found the dining room and hallway without any trouble, and halfway down the hall on my left I found Room Six. I fitted the key into the keyhole and let myself in.

The room was about the same as the one I had had in the Twin Star, with the exception that it had a small closet with shelves instead of a chest of drawers and it had no washstand. I set my bag on the floor of the closet and stretched out on the bed.

I could not say that I liked this place at all, but I was stuck in it. As long as I was chatting with the Gridleys in the front room, it seemed like sport. But now that I had my horse out of reach and was enclosed in this little room, I began to think of all the things I didn't like the looks of. Not least among them was the key itself. It was such a common sort that I could imagine everyone on the premises having one just like it, and anyone from Tim to Norma could let himself in at any hour of the day or night. Of the four adults, I did not trust a one of them, and I did not have the glimmering of an idea of how I was going to gather intelligence. I was going to have to be on my guard and not tip my hand, which meant not asking very many direct questions.

I made myself imagine scenarios in which I slipped up. In one, Mr. Gridley asked me how the weather had been in Laramie recently. In another, he asked me what some of the main outfits were that had horses running out on the Red Desert. In another, he asked me if I wanted to take a bath, and I told him, no, I just had one last night. He asked, where was that?

I got up off the bed and looked under it. I saw nothing there but dust and a couple of fuzz balls. I went to the window and looked out at a chokecherry hedge I hadn't noticed earlier when I took the horse around. Thinking ahead about how I would do things when I went to bed that night, I set the wooden chair tilted against the door.

Still restless, I took my bag out of the closet and set it on the bed. I took out my coat and set it aside, then unrolled my gunbelt and pulled my six-shooter out of its holster. I clicked the cylinder around, made sure the hammer was down on an empty chamber, and put the gun away. For a moment I wished I hadn't left my rifle in its scabbard, strapped to my saddle, but then as I thought things out I realized I wasn't likely to have a gun battle with these people. As long as I didn't make a show of money and didn't act snoopy, they would probably humor me at a dollar a day.

As I was putting things back in my bag, I noticed that the top button on my coat was about to come off. For as much as it was a nuisance to have to sew on a button, I knew it was best to take care of it while I had the time. Leaving the coat on the bed and putting the bag on the closet floor, I went out to look for some needle and thread.

The place seemed to be empty up front. I had to stand around and call out for several minutes until Norma appeared and asked, in a rough voice, if I needed something.

I asked for a needle and thread, and before I had a chance to say what color I'd like, Norma turned and left. A couple of minutes later I had a spool of heavy black thread with a two-inch needle stuck through the strands.

Back in the room, I took the trouble to cut and pull out the old thread, and then I sewed on the button good and strong. I tried on the coat, saw that everything worked fine, then put it away and went out to look for Norma.

I found Mr. Gridley instead, sitting on a stool behind the reception desk. I thanked him for the needle and thread, which he took with his usual smile. As he set it on the counter he asked me a question.

"How long have you been in Wyoming, Jimmy?"

"Not very long, really."

"I bet you've seen a lot of places."

"A few." I realized he was fishing for more, so I said, "I was down in Pueblo before I came to work on this job."

"Lookin' for horses there, too?"

I laughed. "No, on that job I was lookin' for saddles."

He tipped his head in the way that people have of expressing, "Well, how about that?"

"It's all work," I said.

"It sure is."

Before any silence could set in, I said, "I think I might go out and stretch my legs a bit. Walk uptown."

"Plenty of time."

"See what there is to see. What about the place across the road, by the way?"

"The Falconer? Oh, it's a fancy place compared to this one. A little too rich for our blood, but a fine place all the same, I'm sure. Were you looking for something?"

"Oh, no. Just thinkin' about goin' out and seein' a few things."

At that moment, Norma came through the swinging door, the beady eyes roving.

"Thanks for the needle and thread," I offered in what I hoped was a friendly tone.

"Any time," came the answer from the host.

Taking in the two of them, I said, "I think I'll go out now and stretch my legs, as I said."

Mr. Gridley nodded as he handed the needle and thread to Norma. "You bet, Jimmy. See you at suppertime."

With a smile for both of them, I turned and walked to the door. Even if it was rich for their blood, I thought I'd like to take a gander at the place across the road.

CHAPTER SIX

The Falconer House had a great air of respectability, with its solid-looking timbers well fitted and joined. The very materials spoke of effort and expense. The surrounding plains for miles around were treeless, and even in an oasis like Raven Springs, the trees were of the common and soft variety—from chokecherry, which could hardly be called a tree but often was, to scrubby box elder and then elm and cottonwood. For anything more substantial than a chicken roost, the people who built the businesses and houses here would have had to freight in the lumber. I would guess that the nearest sawmill lay thirty or forty miles to the south, almost into Colorado. Whoever owned the Falconer House, then, valued a good impression.

I lifted the latch, and the thick door swung inward without a creak. I stepped inside and listened, but I could not hear a sound. Two more steps took me through the entryway into a dim reception area, and if it hadn't been for the fireplace and leather chairs, I might have thought I had wandered into a museum that was closed for the day. Straight ahead of me, the reception desk was flanked on each side by a mounted bird that I took to be a falcon. The one on the left sat on a perch with his head lifted and turned to his right, so that his glass eye greeted whoever came in. The bird on the right, suspended by two wires from an overhead beam, had his wings out and his claws opened as if he was swooping to his prey. A few feet to the right of this fierce-looking specimen, standing in wisdom on a thick shelf built out from the wall, was a great horned owl who stared ahead with glassy yellow eyes. Past him, in the center of the mantel over the stone fireplace, a well-groomed red-tailed hawk stood in profile. As I turned to see the rest of the room, my gaze went upward to the two corners. In each one, on a dark wooden corner shelf, sat a bird that was probably some other species of falcon but that, in an outdoor place, I would have taken for a common chicken hawk.

I stood in this quiet company for upward of a minute, wondering if Jeanette and Penny had gone back to the inn and wondering also if a proprietor or any hired help were about. I brought my gaze back across the room, noting the overhead chandelier this time as well as an oak wall clock with a hinged glass window and a brass winding key on the inside ledge. I also observed a dark-stained door that was set in the wall between the suspended bird and the stately owl, and a larger, lighter-colored, double door on the far wall to my right, which I presumed led into a dining room. I decided to call out.

"Yoo-hoo! Anyone home?" I waited half a minute and repeated my call.

Another long moment passed until I heard footsteps on a wooden floor. They seemed to be headed toward the small door I had noticed a couple of minutes earlier. As I waited, the doorknob turned, the dark door opened inward, and a man stepped through.

He closed the door behind him and adjusted his cuffs as he took his place behind the counter. My first impression was that his hair was too perfectly in place. He had dark brown hair and a matching full mustache, trimmed straight across on the bottom to give him a firm, authoritative look. He had dark brown eyes as well, and a full set of gleaming white teeth, which he showed with a smile.

"Good afternoon. May I help you with something? A room for the night?"

"Actually, I already have arrangements. I'm staying at the inn across the road. But your place is so nice-looking that I thought I would come over and admire it."

"Oh, well, you're certainly welcome to."

"Thank you. I'm glad I came. This is high-class to me."

"Why, thank you. That's very flattering." He reached into his coat, took out a leather cigarette case, opened it, and lifted out a tailor-made. He stuck the cigarette in his mouth and put the case back inside his coat. Then he reached under the counter and came out with a match, which he struck. As he lit the cigarette, he said, "Traveling far?"

"I'm on my way to the Red Desert, to look for stray horses."

"Oh, uh-huh." He shook out the match.

"My name's Jimmy Clevis," I said, stepping forward and holding out my hand. "I can't get over what a swell place you've got here."

He set the dead match on the counter top and gave me his hand. "Samuel Frye." He smiled again and showed his white teeth, then took back his hand as if it was not his custom to let it out for very long. As he lifted his chin and took a drag on the cigarette, I noticed his Adam's apple. He blew out the smoke, then lowered his head to look my way. "Did you have anything else in mind? There's really not much to see around here."

"Nothin' in particular. Just killin' time until supper."

"Well, I'm glad you came over. Always enjoy meeting new people."

"Thanks," I said. Looking to my right and left, I added, "Well, I guess I'll move on. Not trouble you any longer. But I appreciate being able to see your place."

He smiled again. "No trouble at all."

I turned around to head for the door, and my attention was caught by yet another bird, this one on a shelf to the right of the entryway. I believe it was the biggest dead bird in the lodge, standing about a foot and a half tall and glaring at me with his glass eyes. I had the quick sensation that he had been watching me all that time. In a glance I took in the sharp, curved beak, the wings lifted halfway out, and the legs that were feathered all the way down to the claws. I pivoted to look at Mr. Frye, who seemed to be watching me as I left.

"He's a nice one. What kind of bird is he?"

"Goshawk."

"Beautiful."

"Isn't he, though?" Mr. Frye smiled beneath a cloud of smoke.

"Sure is." I opened the heavy front door and walked out of the Falconer House into the bright sunlight.

Now that I had seen the Empire Inn and the Falconer House, I stepped into the road between them and headed toward town proper. A light afternoon breeze played through the leaves of the cottonwoods and elms and carried the sound of a barking dog. Then I caught a whiff of woodsmoke, which on a warm afternoon suggested to me that someone was baking bread or pies. Of course, some less benign person could be boiling water to scrape a hog or scald chickens, but I preferred to think of the more pleasant alternative. It reminded me of relaxed afternoons when I rode into Chanate and Magdalena's neighborhood and knew that the good señoras of the town were rolling out tortillas and stirring dark pots.

The town itself seemed somewhat innocent, again from the outside, after I had gone through the passage of what now seemed like the Scylla and Charybdis for travelers to Raven Springs. As I approached the first houses, I saw a little girl in front of one of them. She was standing in an unfenced yard, holding a cat almost as large as herself. The cat's front legs were sticking straight up above the girl's hug, and its head peeped up and moved to watch me as I went by. In the side yard of another house, a boy about Ollie's age was stabbing at the ground with what looked like an old bayonet. I walked on, having nothing more to worry about than the thought that Tim might be inspecting the spurs in my saddlebag or that Norma might be clicking the cylinder on my six-gun.

In the middle of town I passed a general store, and through the front window I could see sacks of flour and beans stacked along one wall, a washboard hanging on another wall, and the wicket of the post office in one corner. I walked past a hardware store, a butcher shop, a land and title company, and a doctor's office. The smell of oiled leather reached me through the open door of a saddle and boot shop. On the corner sat a hotel called the Red Coach, which I thought was an elegant name for a wooden building with a window on one side only and an old man sitting in a stuffed chair, drowsing, with a cane wedged upright between his leg and the arm of the chair.

Farther down the street I could see what looked like a saloon, a cheap café, and a livery stable, none of which I needed at the moment, so I crossed the main street and walked back in the other direction. On the corner was a dry goods store with bolts of cloth in view, then a druggist's with a mortar and pestle painted on the window, and next a barber shop, where a lean, balding man stood in the doorway and appraised me as I passed. Then came the sheriff's office, with a sturdy-looking log jail in back, and on the corner sat a blacksmith shop. I caught the smell of cinders and heated iron, and I heard the clanking of metal on metal.

Now I stood at the corner, and I realized I had turned around too soon and had gone through the main part of town too fast. So I turned around and headed west again, past the jail and the loitering barber and the apothecary shop, where I imagined an old man in spectacles bent over a bench in a back room, grinding a mysterious white powder.

Down the next block I passed a wagon maker's establishment, which looked mainly like a bone-yard for broken wheels and axles. I went past another stable, this one closed up and chained, and then the office of a drayage company. Across the way I could see the saloon. I kept going west until I came to a few nondescript houses with empty lots in between. I crossed back over to the north side of the street, turned right, and headed back to the center of town.

When I came to the next cross street, I looked to my left before stepping down. There, in front of a dingy little house, I saw something that stopped me.

At the edge of the street, a man stood holding a horse and talking to another man. I could hear voices but couldn't pick up words. The second man was old and heavy, bent over nearly level and leaning on a stick. He had a large, round middle, a thick upper body stretching a pair of suspenders, and a sizeable head with a short-billed cloth cap fitted over bristly white hair. His voice was going up and down, and he was motioning with his free left hand. The other man's voice was low and indistinguishable, and even though he had his back part way turned to me, I knew him at a glance: the flat-crowned hat, shabby sackcloth coat, and denim trousers. I did not have to see the boils on his neck or the milky left eye to know it was Ross Milaham.

Although I recognized his form in an instant, I was puzzled about his reason for being here. When I had seen him earlier on my trip, as I was now sure I had, I thought he might be shadowing me. Now I didn't think so, for I had walked up on him. I could only imagine that he was looking for one of the many lost people whose descriptions he carried in his wallet. Somewhere in the course of almost a week, between Fort Collins and here, he had gotten out on the trail ahead of me. For all I knew, he had ridden up the road between the two inns while I was sewing the button on my coat.

The voice of the old bent-over man rose again as I stepped into the street and headed for the other side. Out of the corner of my eye I kept a watch on the two of them, and just before I stepped up onto the dirt walkway, Milaham shifted in his slouch and cast a glance my way with his better eye. Then he said something to the old man, who started his harangue again.

The livery stable closed me from their view, and I felt a small relief as I walked down the block. I paused outside the saloon, where I heard the undertone of voices, the slap of a leather cup on a bar top, and the rattle of dice. I moved on, steering straight ahead and not looking into the café as I passed it.

As I gained the next block, I saw a man in a straw hat come out of the general store and untie a mule from the rack. He flipped a rein around the off side of the animal's neck, got the two reins together on the saddle horn, and made ready to mount up. Each time he tried, though, the mule would move its hind quarter away from the man and its front quarters toward him. With each false start, the man would stop the animal, reposition himself, and try again. Finally, after almost a complete turn in the middle of the street, he got his foot into the stirrup and swung aboard. As the animal trotted away, I saw that a small package wrapped in brown paper had fallen to the ground.

"Hey," I called out, "you dropped something."

The rider paid no attention.

"Say," I called, louder this time, "you dropped something!"

The rider stopped and turned the mule partway around. I pointed at the package in the street. The man felt the left pocket of his denim jacket, raised his chin, and reined the mule the rest of the way around. As the animal walked toward me, I stepped into the street and picked up the package. The man rode up with me on his right side, and he stopped the mule about a yard from me.

"Is this yours?" I asked, holding the package toward him.

He didn't speak but just gazed at me, and for a moment I thought he might be the village idiot, except that a person in that capacity usually went around on foot, or so I assumed. Even so, this fellow looked dense. He had a large moon face, a dark complexion, and a black mustache. Behind his heavy brows there seemed to be some thoughts in slow motion.

"Is this yours?" I repeated. Then it occurred to me that I could ask him in Spanish. "*¿Es tuyo?*"

A dull glow of comprehension went over him. "*Ah, sí. Son mis dulces. Se me cayeron.*" Oh, yes. They are my candies. They fell from me.

I handed the package closer, and he took it. From then on we spoke in Spanish. He had a sort of mumbling voice, but I followed him all right.

"Do you want one?"

"No, thanks."

"Have one. They're mine. I just bought them."

"No, that's all right."

"They're very good. They taste like lemon." With the package in his hand, he swung down from the saddle. Then he unwrapped the brown paper and held the opened treasure in the palm of his thick hand. "Take one."

I did. It was as hard as a stone, so with my tongue I poked it into the side of my mouth.

He gave a curious laugh, somewhere between hesitant and apologetic, and took a candy for himself.

"Do you live here?" I asked.

He went on to tell me how he worked on a ranch for a boss named Fron-kleen, which I interpreted to be Franklin. He took care of cattle and horses. Franklin was a very good boss. His wife died on him, and he liked to drink. He spoke Spanish and was very good with a rifle. He ate meat every day, always beef.

"And you, what's your name?"

"Chilo," he said. I could imagine Tome flattening it out to Chee-loe.

"My name's Jimmy," I said. "My friends call me Yimi. Do you come to town often?"

He gave his little laugh again. "Some days. To buy candy."

"That's good. You don't go looking for the girls?" I motioned with my head toward the saloon.

"No, they are very ugly."

"Yes. Isn't that true? So how long have you worked for this Señor Franklin?"

"A few years. He is very good." From there, Chilo moved into a long circumstantial story about a job he had earlier. He mixed mortar for a mason, or *maestro* as he called him. They built a large storehouse out of adobe. The maestro was very good, and he liked to drink also. Red wine. But he worked every day, and they built a house for some other people. Always Chilo mixed the mortar, but he could tell the maestro whenever an adobe was not level. Then another maestro came with his two boys, and they plastered the adobe walls and painted them white. An adobe house was much better in hot weather or cold, not like these poor houses made of wood. But here they made all the houses of wood.

"That is true," I said. "Do you know the inn, the one that is made with wood of better quality?" I motioned with my head in that direction.

"Oh, yes. With the birds of prey. They are all very pretty. I had the chance to go in there one time. Their eyes are all made of glass. Isn't that right?"

"That's what I understand. Do you know the owner?"

"Just barely. He was very friendly."

"Is he a friend of your boss?"

"They know each other. They talked about some business. When the señora died, Franklin had to sell some things. They left me to look at the birds."

"Does he wear a wig?"

"Franklin?"

"No, the man with the dead birds."

Chilo gave his hesitant laugh. "I don't know. I didn't notice."

Then he told me how the birds always died in the water tanks, especially the little crows and magpies when they first learned to fly up onto the edge. From there he launched into a story about how they had once repaired a water tank that had cracked when the ground froze. I understood that he mixed the mortar for that job, too, but I didn't know if he was working for Franklin at that time, or the maestro, or someone else in some other time and place. He went on to tell of a cold winter, with much snow and icicles a meter in length, and at the New Year they had a dance. Women came from all the ranchos, and pretty girls, and when the dance was over the men went outside and tramped down all the snow so that the women could walk to the wagons and carriages.

"Oh. Did Franklin go to that dance?"

"Oh, no. It was over there in el Rancho Golondrinas."

"And where is that?"

"Over there in New Mexico."

"And what was the maestro's name?"

"Lalo."

"Did he work with stone?"

"Oh, yes. Stone, brick, adobe. He did good work, and the houses are better there."

"And the girls?"

He laughed again, in his uncertain way. "At the dances, there were many. But their fathers and their brothers were always there, very jealous."

"Wasn't there one that filled your eye?"

"I don't know."

"But they are prettier than the ones from here."

He glanced in the direction of the saloon. "These are very ugly."

"And how about the sister of the owner of the other inn?" I motioned again in the direction of the two roadhouses. "Is she a witch?"

He laughed, plainer now. "*Solterona, molacha.*" Old maid, woman with a missing tooth.

"How about the girl who works there?"

"*¿La niña?*"

"Yes, the little girl."

"She never goes out. They watch her very well." A sly look crept across his face. "Do you like her?"

"She's pretty young, don't you think?"

"Oh, yes, but if you like her . . ."

"I'm not very interested. I'm just staying there for the night, and they strike me as curious people. A little odd."

"Maybe they are."

"Does Franklin know them?"

"I don't know what for."

"That's true. How many horses do you care for?"

"Between ten and fifteen. Twelve right now."

"And cattle?"

He laughed, shrugging his shoulders. "I don't know. A thousand."

"How many mules?"

"Just two. This one and an old one."

"Who sells mules around here, then?"

"Oh, in Rawlins. Are you looking to buy some?"

"No, not me. I just like to know things. Like where the girls are. I would like to go to one of those dances, but it is too far away."

"Oh, yes."

"If you want to throw your money away, you can find the ugly ones anywhere. But the good ones, that's harder."

He nodded, with something of a leer on his face.

"So tell me, what does Franklin shoot? He doesn't hunt for meat if he eats beef every day."

Chilo said something I couldn't understand. It sounded like "predator," but there's not a word close to that in Spanish, and it didn't make sense.

"What's that?"

"The little squirrels that live in their caves in the ground."

"Oh, prairie dogs," I said in English.

"*Sí, sí.* Preddi doe."

"Does he drink good whiskey?"

He laughed in his odd way. "I don't know."

It seemed to me that talking to Chilo was somewhat like sewing a button on a coat. You went in one hole and came out another, with no set pattern and no determined place to end. At some point you tied it off and cut the thread, and that was what I decided to do. I looked up and down the main street. We had been standing in the middle of it for several minutes, and no one else had come by.

"Chilo," I said, "it's a pleasure to meet you." I gave him my hand.

"Much pleasure in meeting you. If you come by here, look for me at the ranch of el Señor Franklin, and there you will find me, at your service."

"Very well. May it all go well for you."

"The same to you. May you have a good trip, and learn many things."

"Thank you."

"You like to shoot preddi doe?"

"Not so much. I'd rather drink the whiskey."

He leaned back his head and laughed.

"Maybe we'll go to a dance some day, the two of us."

He smiled. "With the girls."

"That's right."

He stood in the middle of the street, with the open package of candy still in his hand, as I turned and walked away.

On my way back to the inn now, I crossed the main street so that I wouldn't walk past the same houses as I did when I walked into town. I made an effort not to look in back of me or very much to either side. When I had straightened out my route and had gone about a block, I heard hoofbeats coming up behind me at a fast walk. Thinking that it might be Chilo with some afterthought, I looked over my left shoulder. I saw Ross Milaham on the brown horse he had been holding earlier. As he came up beside me, I stopped and faced him. He brought the horse to a halt and looked down at me.

"What do you want?" I asked.

"I might ask the same of you."

"My wants are simple, and they don't have much to do with you."

His hand went to his side, to touch the pistol butt through the material of his coat. "I'll put it to you straight, then. I don't like to think you're following me."

"Then don't."

With both hands on the saddle horn, he bore down on me now with his one good eye. "Are you lookin' for your Mexican friend, then?"

"I don't see where that would matter, even if I was."

"Well, I'm not. So don't think I'm gonna lead you to him."

"I would hardly think that."

"Just wanted to make it clear. I don't like to be followed."

I raised my eyebrows. "You may have been that important with someone in the past, who knows who, but in this case you're not."

"Then why have you been askin' about me?"

I had to think fast. I had asked different people for different reasons, and I didn't feel like mentioning Dr. McCabe or Ben Grimes here in the middle of the street. I answered, "Because I thought I saw you in Fort Collins."

"So what if you did?"

"As you might understand, I don't like to be followed either."

"Well, aren't we smart? It's just as if we understood each other." He shifted his hands and touched his coat again. "Let me tell you this, Mister Snoop. You stay clear of me, and I'll do the same for you."

"Good enough. Just to make it easy for you to do your part, I'll tell you where I'm staying. Right down there, in the Empire. The one with two stories."

"Hah! Don't worry about that. You wouldn't catch me dead in that place."

"Good," I said. "I wouldn't want to."

"Fine with me. And a word to the wise. It would be in your best interests not to be throwin' my name around any more. And if you run into me, you'd just as well let on you don't know me."

"That's fine, too. And I'll trust you to return the compliment."

CHAPTER SEVEN

On my way back to the inn, I mulled over the last two conversations I had had. Milaham must have seen me talking to Chilo, and he may have picked up our speaking in Spanish. If he put that together with the meeting he and I had in Chanate's patio, he should be satisfied that I was looking for Fernando. Whatever Milaham was looking for, he must have decided, as I had, that it would be best not to tip one's hand in Raven Springs.

For my own part, I didn't think it would have been that difficult to slip in a question about Fernando when I was talking with Chilo. Even though it would have been in Spanish and probably not understood beyond the two of us, I was not yet ready to state my true business to anyone here. Chilo, who seemed indiscriminate as to what he talked about and with whom, might have put my business on the street in a matter of minutes. That could wait. If I wanted to talk to him again, I thought I knew where I could find him—with some ranchman who had either the first or the last name of Franklin. And from what I understood, Chilo liked to come into town with some frequency. I wouldn't blame him for wanting a little variety from living on a ranch where a widower boss drank whiskey and shot prairie dogs.

As I walked up the steps to the Empire Inn, I heard voices inside. One of them, deep and boisterous, sounded familiar, so I was not taken much by surprise when I walked into the reception area and saw Ben Grimes sitting at the dining room table. Even if I had not heard his voice, I would have recognized him by his gray wool overshirt, which had not gotten any cleaner since the last time I had seen him.

He was seated across from the innkeeper, who had his arms folded on his chest and was smiling with his mouth closed. A bottle of whiskey sat on the table midway between the two men.

Mr. Gridley raised his hand and waved me in. "C'm here, Jimmy, and meet another man."

I went in and stood at the end of the table. "Hello," I said.

Grimes looked at me with a relaxed expression in his large wide eyes. "Are you the other fella stayin' here?"

"That I am."

He turned in his seat and held out his large hand. "Ben Grimes."

"Jimmy Clevis," I said as we shook.

"Well," said our host, "did you get a good look at our town, Jimmy?"

"I'd say I did, such as it is."

"Not much to it, is there?"

"Not unless I missed something."

"Have a drink," said Grimes, "and tell us about yourself."

"There's not much to know about me," I answered.

"Have a seat anyway. Landlord, can we have another glass?"

"Sure." Mr. Gridley got up, went to a shelf on the wall, and came back with a tumbler. He set it in front of me as I took my seat.

Grimes poured me enough for a Methodist preacher, and then he topped off the other two drinks. "Here's how," he said, raising his glass. "Here's to 'em. Them that can, and them that cain't."

We all touched our glasses. I took a sip and watched Mr. Gridley as he puckered his mouth, drawing his whiskers in, and then wet his lips.

Grimes's voice came booming out of his beard. "So what do you do, Jimmy? It's Jimmy, isn't it?"

"It sure is. Right now I'm on a job looking for lost horses. Out in the Red Desert. And yourself?"

"I'm a freighter. A two-fisted, mule-skinnin' sonofabitch."

I looked at Mr. Gridley, who was forcing a tight-lipped smile.

"I been all over," Grimes went on. "Seen a lot of things."

"I imagine."

"If it can be done, I've prob'ly tried it. Drunk every liquor known to man, and tried just about every kind of woman."

"How many kinds are there?" I asked.

"Ha, ha, ha! You put it that way, and they're all the same. They've all got that same little thing." He pushed his hat back on his head. "But I think you know what I mean. There's yer black girls and the yaller ones, yer Indian girl with her red socks, yer Mexican girl, then these immigrant girls, Swedes an' such, that don't know what a douche is for—"

"Keep it down a little," said Mr. Gridley, who had been wincing through this last topic. "The women are right here in the kitchen, and I think they'll be serving supper pretty soon."

"Oh," said Grimes. "Sometimes a fella forgets."

"It's all right. But you know how women can be. Delicate."

"Oh, sure. White women, that is. You take redskins, now, their women can go out and scalp a man, or cut off his thang, or peel his hide off in quarter-inch strips, and not think a thing about it."

"Have you seen some of that?" I asked.

"Some of it," he said with a hard stare. "I tell ya, I've seen a lot of things. A hell of a lot. And not just by Indians. No, sir. I've driven my wagons right through a thousand sheep that had all been clubbed to death, and I've seen white men pleased as punch to have their picture taken with men they've shot full of holes. I've even seen 'em pull on the legs of a man they didn't string up good enough. Legs kickin', and these other two grabbin' on his ankles like a coupla monkeys. I'll tell ya, the things I've seen, why, my life would make a good book. And every bit of it is true."

"Tell me one thing, then," said Mr. Gridley. "Something I've heard but I've never seen it, and I wonder if it's true."

"What's that?"

"Have you ever seen a man knock down a steer with one punch?"

"Oh, yeh. Hit 'em in the neck just right. I've done it." Grimes took out his tobacco and papers, and with his head raised in an attitude of authority, he rolled himself a smoke. Before lighting it he offered the makin's to both Mr. Gridley and me, and we each thanked him but passed.

All this time I could hear the sounds of people working in the kitchen, and I was not surprised when Norma came through the door carrying a cutting board with a knife and two loaves of bread on it.

I pushed my chair back with my legs as I stood up. "I should take a seat over there, don't you think?"

Mr. Gridley shrugged. "Either way. You're the only two guests so far, so we've got plenty of space." He looked up at Norma, who was going back into the kitchen, and then he moved to take the chair I had been sitting in. I hung my hat on a peg and took a seat on the other side of Grimes, who kept his hat on.

Norma came into the room again with a platter of fried potatoes, and the smell of hot grease came wafting through the doorway.

"Startin' to look good," Grimes announced, lifting his nose at the platter.

The landlord smiled in his close-mouthed way. Then he said, "We eat good here."

Penny came in with the tableware and set a plate, a knife, a fork, and a spoon in front of each of us. Then she set four other places and slipped back into the kitchen.

Norma made another appearance, this time with a platter heaped with fried pieces of beef. Again I caught the hot kitchen smell as well as that of cooked meat. As Norma stuck a serving fork into the meat, I thought here was a person who probably always had a skillet full of hot grease on hand.

I had begun to wonder where Jeanette was, and

before long she came in from the hallway with little Ollie in tow. She took a seat at the second place from the corner, and the boy went two places farther down, to the last place on the side across from Grimes and me, and inched his way onto the chair. When he looked up I smiled.

Penny brought in a pitcher of water, set it on the table, turned and took four glasses off the shelf, set them out, and took a seat between Jeanette and Ollie. Through it all I thought she kept her head turned away from Mr. Gridley, but I couldn't be sure.

Norma came through the door one more time, beating a heavy metal spoon against the lip of a pot. I craned my neck a little and saw that the pot had gravy in it. Norma sat down in the remaining seat between Mr. Gridley and Jeanette.

"Go ahead and dig in," said the host. "Guests first."

"Oh, women first," insisted Grimes. "Women and children."

I watched as everyone took food from the platters. After Penny served Ollie, Grimes and I helped ourselves. I had told myself to keep an eye on the food and how it was served, but from the way everyone partook freely, I let my worries go and settled in to enjoy the meal.

Grimes, meanwhile, had not given up on his role as the central entertainer. He plied the kids with such jokes as "What room can nobody enter? A mushroom!" and "Do you know why there are so many people named Smith in this country? Well, when I was back east, I found out the answer. I saw a Smith Manufacturing Company." After a blank stare from Ollie each time, he directed his next joke to the table at large.

"So there was a fella that had a barber shop, and every Saturday afternoon, when he was busiest, the same man would stick his head in the door and say, 'Looks like you're pretty busy. How long do you think it'll be?' And the barber looks around at all the people waitin', and he says, 'Oh, at least an hour and a half,' and the fella answers, 'Good. Thanks.' This goes on for about three Saturdays in a row, and finally the barber says to one of the loafers hangin' around in there, he says, 'Hey, why don't you go follow that joker and see where he goes?' In a little while the loafer comes back, and the barber says, 'Did you see where he went?' 'Sure did,' says the loafer. 'Well, where did he go?' And the loafer says, 'Yer house.'"

The kids didn't even look up. Jeanette managed a little "Heh, heh, heh," but Mr. Gridley and Norma showed no reaction at all. Mr. Gridley called for the water pitcher and poured himself a glassful to set beside his whiskey glass. Norma sat stone-faced.

Grimes did not seem daunted. After a couple of mouthfuls of food, he began to talk about how much he liked music. It was surprising, he said, that in even the most out-of-the-way places, he would meet someone who played an instrument or sang as fine as any minstrel.

Mr. Gridley said that he was thinking of getting a piano sometime in the next year or so if he could afford it, and maybe he could bring someone in to teach the girl how to play it. I glanced at Penny, who did not look up from her plate.

Grimes directed a joke at Ollie. "Tell me, boy, how do you keep from getting hungry if you get locked in a room with nothing but a calendar?" When he got no answer, he said, "Eat the dates off the calendar!" After another silence he added, "You see, dates are a kind of fruit."

He ate for another minute, slowly as I had noticed before, and then he addressed the boy again. "I was just tryin' you out on that last one. What do you do if you get locked in a room with nothing but a piano?" The boy stared at him. "Why, you take a key from the piano and unlock the door with it! Ha, ha, ha! Don't you get it? The keys are the black and white things you press down on to get the music."

Grimes took a drink from his glass of whiskey and smiled around at the others at the table. "One more," he said. "If nobody minds."

Jeanette nodded, holding her lips closed on a mouthful she had just taken in.

"There was a fellow who got a piano for his wife, and after a couple of months a friend of his asked him how everything was going. The man said, 'Well, she's learned to play the piano all right, but she always has to sing along with it, and I can't stand the way she sings. I don't know what to do about it.' And his friend says, 'I know another fella that had the same problem, and he solved it.' 'Is that right?' says the man. 'What did he do?' 'He sold the piano and bought his wife a flute.'"

Grimes took to laughing at his own joke, and Jeanette let out with a little laugh. Mr. Gridley, though, looked as if he was having to force a smile, and Norma sat tight-jawed.

After that, no one spoke for several minutes, and all I heard was the clatter of forks and knives against the crockery of the plates. Ollie slurped his water, and Penny gave him a stern look. A couple of minutes later, I glanced down the table to see all three adults motionless at the same time. Mr. Gridley had finished eating and was leaning on one elbow, Norma was holding up a napkin with both hands, and Jeanette had paused with her left index finger in the corner of her eye. Just for a second, I thought they might make a good version of the three wise monkeys—hear no evil, speak no evil, and see no evil. The instant passed when Norma lowered the napkin and Jeanette finished rubbing her eye, and then I saw, as before, three hardened people exerting an effort to seem hospitable.

Norma set down the napkin, pushed away from the table, stood up, and went into the kitchen. I wondered if there was a plate of apple fritters coming up.

Jeanette turned to her left. "Hurry up, kids, and get the table cleared."

When Penny stood up and started gathering dishes, I figured the evening meal was over. A quietness had fallen on the room, and I didn't think it had much to do with the guests. I didn't have any reason to want to go to my room, though, and I was interested to see what further conversation might come out between Grimes and our host, so I sat in my chair and took a drink from my whiskey glass.

Grimes took out his makin's again, and as he made himself a smoke I noticed that he wasn't quite as smooth as before. His thick, calloused hands seemed to labor now as he brought the two edges of the paper together, rolled the cigarette, licked the seam, and tapped it. His movements made me wonder how much of his talkativeness was an act and how much of it might be the whiskey getting to him.

At this point Mr. Gridley reached around the corner of the table to the place where Norma had sat, and opening a drawer, he took out a long-stemmed pipe and a pouch of tobacco. He stuffed the bowl and lit it, and as he did so it seemed to me that he was assuming the air of the person who sits at the head of the table. After he had puffed out a couple of clouds of smoke, he set the dead match on the table and looked at Grimes.

"Well, tell me, Ben," he said. "What sort of freight do you haul?"

"Mostly goods and supplies."

"Wouldn't that cover just about everything?"

"Not if you know the business. For example, I don't haul ore, or coal, or salt. That's another kind of haulin', shorter distances, with more teams and slow goin'. Me, I'm more the type to go from one place to another. I'll bring in a load of grub on one wagon, like flour and beans and salt and molasses, and a load of hardware in another, like a keg of nails, a roll of bcb wire, you name it. Canvas, washtubs, rope, anything down to a set of door handles. Then I'll take a load of hides back, or barrels of meat. On another run, I'll have three or four wagons of lumber, and go back loaded with sacks of wheat. Just depends on where it takes me."

"What's the best kind of draft animals, in your opinion?"

"Mules," came the quick answer.

Mr. Gridley puffed his pipe.

"Not just anyone can work around 'em, but you talk to a real mule-skinner, and he'll tell you there's no better way. I've hauled field cannons, steam engines—hell, if you want a piano, I can bring that in and set it down without a nick or scratch. Fact is, me and my partner Lawhorn hauled in a piano and two of the biggest, heaviest mirrors you'll ever see, all the way from Denver to a whorehouse in Lusk." He turned to me. "Maybe you know the place."

"Can't say that I do, but if I'm ever in that town, I'll ask around for it."

"Two wagons, then?" said Mr. Gridley.

"On that trip, yeh. We like to run more when we've got the orders and we can get another driver or two. Like I said, sometimes I'll have three or four wagons."

Mr. Gridley studied him through the smoke. "Is your work kinda thin right now, then?"

Grimes flicked the ash off his cigarette and took a slow drag. "Not so much," he said. "I'm on business right now. Just because I'm not haulin' a load of chamber-pots don't mean I'm not on the job. I work every day, in-season."

"Oh, I'm sure."

"I've got a good business, and I stay busy. And if there's somethin' that needs lookin' after, I do it." Grimes lifted his chin and bushy beard.

"I didn't mean it any other way. I can tell you're a man who looks after things. You wouldn't be where you are if you weren't."

"Meanin'?"

Mr. Gridley shrugged. "Meanin', you've got a prosperous business, and that doesn't happen to a man if he doesn't know what's what. The right hand's got to know what the left hand's doin'."

Grimes took a drink of his whiskey. "I didn't just fall off the turnip wagon."

"No one would think that."

"If there's somethin' needs to be known, I kin find

it out. I'm an old coon that's been up the hill and over the mountain."

Mr. Gridley went sort of pig-eyed as he rested his pipe on the table and made his close-mouthed smile. "I bet you have, Ben. And I bet you know what the girls are like on the other side."

"I might." Grimes brought the cigarette to his mouth again.

"Mind you, I'm not one to inquire into someone else's affairs. A man's business is his own. It's all just somethin' to talk about when we're drinkin' whiskey."

"I suppose."

"What else is there to do?"

"Usually two things come to my mind." Grimes licked his lip where he had taken his cigarette away. "But like you said, it seems like the girls are on the other side of the mountain right now, so it's whiskey and small talk." He turned to me. "Same two things come to your mind, Jimmy?"

"Not necessarily whiskey," I said. "Sometimes I'm partial to beer."

"But we're in agreeance on the second thing." He smiled and showed the remnants of his teeth.

"I think we verified that when we determined how many kinds there were."

"That's right. But where'd we end up on that? Just one kind, or several?"

"I think we had it both ways." Now I took a drink from my whiskey.

Grimes turned to the innkeeper. "Like you say, just somethin' to talk about."

"Sure."

"That's what I like about travelin' around. You

meet more people to talk to. You learn somethin' everywhere you go."

"I imagine."

"And you share what you know."

"All the better."

Grimes raised his chin again and took a pull on his cigarette. "What's the heaviest thing you ever lifted?"

"Oh, I don't know."

"Have you ever lifted a steel drum of kerosene?"

"Can't say that I have."

"Well, I'll tell ya, I have. Twice as heavy as a dead man. Ya lay it on its side, lift it by the lip on each end with just your fingertips, and heft it up into the wagon."

"That's quite a lift."

"You do a lot of it with your legs. I can show you how."

"Well, I'm not sure it's that—"

"Naw, we'll just go outside. I'll show you how to lift the heaviest thing you got."

"That's quite all right. I'll take your word for it." Mr. Gridley took up his pipe, palmed the bowl, and got some smoke out of it.

"But you hit the nail on the head earlier. The right hand's got to know what the left one's doin'."

"Uh-huh."

"People take me for a dummy."

"I don't think anyone here does."

"That's just as well." Grimes poured himself more whiskey and fell silent for a moment.

I didn't know what to make of his talk. He seemed to be driving at something, and I wasn't sure what it was. I thought he wanted to impress Mr.

Gridley with his savvy and his brute strength, but I thought he was going about it in a belligerent way. More than that, I sensed some kind of antagonism, as if he thought he could needle Mr. Gridley and get an advantage over him that way. Whatever Grimes's motive, the landlord didn't seem to be playing in, and all it was doing to me was make me feel uneasy. I thought Grimes had already said more than he needed to, and if the Gridleys knew anything at all about Lawhorn the missing partner, they would have some idea of what business this teamster was on. So there I sat, nursing my whiskey and dreading that Grimes might say more, with me all the time helpless to do anything about it.

Grimes smoked his cigarette down to the tiniest stub, where he held it with his yellowed thumbnail and fingernail. Then he dropped it on the floor and stepped on it. I watched Mr. Gridley's eyes follow the action and go back to Grimes taking another drink.

"Yep, that's what I like about traveling around. See lots of things, be my own man. If I want to put up at a place, I can do it. I want a woman, same thing. I pay my own way. I pay my drivers good, too."

Mr. Gridley nodded, then rose from his seat with his pipe in his hand. "I'm goin' to see if the women have a pie for you gents."

"I don't care for any," I offered. I didn't want to eat anything unless I saw people from the house taking some of the same, but I didn't know how to convey the idea to Grimes.

The landlord paused at the door. "How about you, Ben?"

"I suppose. Depends on what kind."

"It'll be either mince or apple."

"Oh, that should be all right."

Mr. Gridley went into the kitchen, and Grimes went about building himself another cigarette. With his tongue between his lips, he looked up at me and gave me a wink. Then the door opened, and our host came into the room with a satisfied expression on his face.

"Got some comin' up. Sure you don't want any, Jimmy?"

"No, thanks. I don't have much of a sweet tooth."

Mr. Gridley patted his paunch where it hung over his belt. "Neither do I, but you'd never know it." Then he smiled, and his side whiskers went up.

The door opened again, and Norma appeared with a slab of mince pie on a plate.

"Fork," said Mr. Gridley.

Norma did an about-face, pushed into the kitchen, returned with a fork on the plate, set it in front of Grimes, and retreated, all in a wordless moment.

Grimes did not make a movement toward the pie. He tapped the seam of his new cigarette, lit it, and toyed with his whiskey glass. Mr. Gridley's glance wavered between the pie and the guest who was supposed to eat it.

I was taking another sip of whiskey when Jeanette came into the dining room by way of the reception area. She stood at the corner of the table and gave me a friendly look.

"The children are having a little campfire outside," she said, "and they'd like you to come and join them."

Grimes turned to me. "Go ahead. But let me fill your glass first." He uncorked the bottle and gurgled about half a cup more into my glass.

"I guess so," I said. "Thanks. I"ll be back in a little while, if you men are still here."

"We're in no hurry," said Grimes.

I looked at our host, who had his eyes half-closed and was shaking his head. "Not at all."

I put on my hat, picked up my drink, cast a glance at the pie still sitting untouched on the table, and followed Jeanette out of the room.

She led the way out the front door and around the building to the back. Night was falling, and the cool air was drawing in, so the sight of a little fire in a circle of rocks gave a cheery feeling. The kids were both sitting on wooden crates near the fire, and they looked at me with little curiosity as I took a seat on an unoccupied crate.

Ollie was poking at the fire with a stick, getting the end ablaze, then pulling the stick out and blowing on the end to make it glow.

"Do you like a campfire?" I asked him.

He gazed at the flames. "I guess."

I looked at Penny, who was also firing the end of a stick. "You must like the fire," I said.

"It's something to do."

"Here," said Jeanette, handing me a stick. "Get the end of it glowing, and then we write words in the air."

I set my whiskey glass on the corner of the crate and crouched forward. I took in the warmth of the fire as I poked the end of the stick into the coals.

Ollie started waving his stick around, and it came within a couple of inches of my nose.

"Don't get too close there," I said.

Jeanette's voice came up from in back of me. "Try to write letters, Ollie. Don't just wave it around."

Now Penny drew her stick out of the heart of the

fire and swirled it across the space in front of her. It
looked as if she was writing her name.

I settled back on my heels and took a drink of
whiskey while my stick heated. Jeanette knelt at my
right and smiled at me, her face and hair shining in
the firelight. She produced another stick and pushed
the end of it into the center of the fire.

Ollie got his stick glowing again and started making O's. Penny wrote something that I couldn't deci-
pher. I rotated my stick.

I don't think I drank all that much whiskey all
that fast, but the next while is a blur to me. The night
closed in darker, and it seemed as if our little campfire was miles away from anyone else. Ollie was getting more animated, dancing around as he wrote
letters in the air and shouted, "Chop yo' head off!
Chop yo' head off!" Penny kept her seat, as I remember, and she wrote things short and close. Then I
joined in, waving my stick and writing letters. I was
standing up, hopping from one foot to the other,
making faces and trying to get Ollie to laugh. I think
Penny smiled but Ollie didn't.

I cavorted around some more, and Jeanette was
on her feet, smiling with her mouth closed, raising
her eyebrows. The two of us swirled our sticks and
wrote things back and forth. I remember thinking
she was very nice after all, and not that bad-looking
in the firelight. She smiled, and I smiled, and we
danced and wrote things in the air. I thought we
were using the same language. I don't know how
much of the whiskey I drank, and I don't know
when the curtain came down.

CHAPTER EIGHT

I woke up in a woman's bed. Daylight was filtering into the room. I did not know whose bed it was, or where. I was lying on my side, facing away from the center of the bed, but I knew it was a woman's. It was clean, and it had a faint perfumed smell. I couldn't remember how I had gotten there or what I had done, but I had some idea of the latter as I had all my clothes off.

My head felt woozy, detached from the rest of me. I felt paralyzed, as if I was chained to the floor, though I was under the covers of a soft bed. I tried to remember events from the night before—Jeanette smiling, waving the lit stick like a wand. Penny looking up and smiling as well, Ollie poking at the fire and scattering the embers.

My head felt as if it had been cut off and was floating. I had a swollen feeling of thirst and nausea at the back of my throat. From where I lay I could see things in the dim light—my boots on the floor, my clothes on a chair, my hat farther away on the floor. I came back to myself. My legs were drawn up, and my right hand touched my knee. I knew I was all in one piece, together. A feeling of dread ran through my whole body. I had done something, and I wanted to keep my back to it.

I felt a body shift on the mattress behind me. I knew I was going to have to turn and look. I wished I could glide off the bed and onto the floor, into my clothes, and out the door, all fluid and horizontal. But I knew I couldn't. I remembered a female form, swaying in the firelight. I had a pretty good idea whose bed it was. I didn't think it was Penny's. I was going to have to face it.

I hunched my shoulders and drew my knees up higher. If only I could go back to sleep and wake up somewhere else. But I needed to get back to my own room.

I straightened out and rolled over. I saw the pale shoulder of a woman, a light-colored head of hair. Then she turned, and I saw the wrinkled, sagging face of an old hag with a tooth missing. It jolted me, scared the hell out of me.

Stray hairs were hanging in front of her face, and she was smiling. Her mouth looked like the whirlpool where sailors disappeared in the story. I remembered another woman, not so long ago, in Pueblo, who looked like that, and I had been able to stay away. But this time she had sucked me right into her. I had to get out.

"Did you wake up?" she asked in a low voice.

"I feel like hell," I whispered.

"Poor baby. You drank a lot."

I wondered about that. "I must have. Did I babble?"

"Just a little. You said you like to get your wick

trimmed." She reached down to touch me and pursed her lips as she smiled. "Do you want to do it again?"

"No," I said, shrinking back. "I need to get back to my own room."

"Don't be in a hurry."

"I need to go."

"Don't worry," she said, patting my hip. "Come back to Mama when you want. Do you remember calling me Mama last night?"

A chill ran through me. Mama spider. "No, I don't."

"You were a big boy, and you liked it."

"Maybe I did, but I've got to go." I was shivering now.

"Go ahead. Come back when you want. Mama'll take you in, the way you like it."

"I've got to find my room."

"Downstairs. There's just the one hallway."

"All right." I slid out of bed and pulled my clothes on. Then I put on my hat and picked up my boots. "Thanks," I whispered from where I stood. I thought I should say that much.

"Sure. And don't worry. Everything's all right."

"So long."

"Good-bye. And don't be afraid to come back."

It seemed like the biggest effort in the world to make myself tread softly as I went down the stairs. On each step I stayed as close to the wall as I could, trying to avoid making the board creak. I was so full of dread that I was sure I was going to stumble, or drop my boots, or holler out in spite of myself. But finally I reached the first floor with no incident, turned into the hallway, and found my room.

Safe inside, I huddled under the covers without taking off my clothes. I felt sick to my very center—rotten with too much whiskey, poisoned by whatever someone had put in my drink, and sick at heart for having fallen so low. In my life I had done a lot of things that I regretted in the morning, but this one loomed as the worst. With all my being I really, really wished I hadn't done it, but I knew I couldn't change what had happened. I was going to have to face any consequences.

In addition to falling to an old weakness that I thought I was getting some control over, I felt I had made a mess out of the job I was supposed to be doing. I wondered how Grimes had fared. Here I had been worried about how he had gotten careless with drink, and I had done the same—and worse, unless he had ended up in the hay with Norma, which I very much doubted.

I couldn't get it out of my head what a bad, bad business I had fallen into. There was everything wrong with it. I had made a big mistake, and I sensed that there was more to it than I yet knew. I was going to have to put things back together, little by little, beginning with whatever impressions I could get from Grimes before I had a chance to talk with him on our own.

Nervous, restless, on edge—I knew I wasn't going to get any more rest, so I threw off the covers and got up. I was going to have to put a good face on things at the breakfast table and see where to go from there.

When I made my appearance in the dining room, I found Mr. Gridley drinking a cup of coffee by himself. When I asked about the other lodger, he told me that Grimes had already checked out and left.

"Really?" I asked.

"Sure enough. He got up early, had a quick breakfast, and pulled out. He seemed like he was anxious to get where he was going."

"So he's gone, huh?"

"Long gone. Like a turkey through the corn. Have some coffee?"

"Um, sure." The news had stunned me, and in my dull state I was slow to take it in. I could not believe Grimes would have just gone on before he found a chance to talk to me, but I had no idea of where he might be or how I might go about looking for him.

Norma appeared with a coffee pot and a cup. With the sensation of being behind a plate of glass, I watched the steaming dark liquid flow into my cup and then into Mr. Gridley's. I could drink the coffee.

A few minutes later, Ollie and Penny came trooping in and sat in the same seats as the night before. Norma brought out a stack of plates and handed them around, then came back with a platter of hotcakes. After the man of the house and the children had dug in, I did so myself. A jar of molasses went around, and the four of us fell to eating.

"Well, Jimmy," said the proprietor in his cheerful tone, "what are your plans for today?"

"I think I'll have to take my horse out and see first. If he's slow at all, I might want to lay over another day. And to tell you the truth, I don't feel much like doing anything today."

"Under the weather a little?"

"I'd say so. I must have had more than I realized. I

sure can't drink like that teamster fellow. I'm surprised he was up and around so early."

"Didn't seem to bother him much. He must be used to it."

I shivered as I shook my head. "If I don't get that way again for a long time, it'll be fine with me."

Mr. Gridley gave a broad smile that made his side whiskers poke out. "No harm done," he said.

After breakfast I went out to the stable to see about my horse. Tim was loitering around the door, smoking a cigarette in the morning sunlight.

"Are yuh movin' on today?" he asked.

"I don't know. I need to take my horse out and see how he is. And I don't feel so good myself."

He stood aside and let me go through the doorway. Inside, I saw no evidence of anything that might have belonged to Grimes. Although I hadn't seen his horse and outfit before, there wasn't much inside the stable to overlook. Mine was the only horse, and the same went for my saddle and the things still tied on it, like my bedroll and rifle scabbard. The stable was not very large, with half a dozen stalls against the far wall, a pile of loose hay on the right with a pitchfork stuck in it, a grain box nearer to me, and a shovel and wheelbarrow crusted with manure. A horse collar hung on the right wall, as did an assortment of trace chains, harness leather, britching, and a singletree. A layer of dust lay on all the old gear, and I formed the impression that the Gridleys did not keep any horses themselves.

I brushed my horse and looked him over, then saddled and bridled him. As I did so, I became aware that Tim had come into the stable behind me.

He closed off the sunlight when he passed through the door, and then he stood by the haystack.

I looked over my shoulder at him. "That other fellow pulled out already, eh?"

"Yuh-huh. He left early."

"Said he was a mule-skinner. Knew a lot of jokes. Good for a barrel of laughs."

"Uh-huh."

"I had a little poem that I heard a while back and wanted to recite for him. I didn't think of it last night, but it came to me this morning, and now I can't get it out of my head."

Tim gave a short, dry cough.

"It goes like this.

> *There was a young fellow named Hyde.*
> *Who fell down a privy and died.*
> *His unfortunate brother*
> *Then fell down another,*
> *And now they're interred side by side."*

Tim showed no response at all, and I didn't have Grimes's talent for explaining the last line, so silence hung in the air for a second.

"I didn't remember it until this morning," I said.

"Uh-huh."

I led my horse past him and out into the sunlight. As I tightened the cinch, I glanced back and saw Tim coming out of the stable and swiping at the ground with the cane I had seen the day before.

"Well," I said, getting my reins set, "I'm going out on a little ride. Chances are I'll stay over another day."

"Hmh."

I swung into the saddle and moved the horse out onto the road. There in the morning sun, looking innocent, sat the Falconer House. In spite of what Mr. Gridley had said, I thought there was some kind of a link between the two places, but I couldn't get a feeling for it. When I had ridden past the lodge, I stopped the little dark horse and swung down. Making it seem as if I was checking the animal, I stooped at each leg, ran my hand down the shank, and picked up a hoof. Then, walking backwards, I led the horse around in a circle, walked him straight out for thirty yards, and brought him back. All this time I was catching glimpses of the Falconer House and its layout.

Like the Empire Inn, it had a building out back that looked like a stable. It also had a big woodpile, with a stump for a chopping block and an ax stuck in the stump. As I made my observations, I formed a clear idea of the dimensions of the main building and how some of the rooms might lie. The place might well have some secrets inside, but I couldn't connect anything with Grimes. And by now I had decided that if I looked for Grimes, I would be looking for Fernando at the same time.

From the lodge I rode into town and through it, then struck out to the southwest to the highest ground I could see. From there I studied the lay of the land. At first it looked all the same, just rolling hills of grass and sagebrush in all directions. As I deliberated more, I could pick out irregularities—a scarp here, a gully there, a line of higher brush where water might run at some time of the year. It was a lot of country to go out and look over in broad daylight, when anyone could see me snooping, but I figured that if anyone had sneaked out to stash a body, he would be sticking close to his regular routine today so as not to look conspicuous. Sooner or later, though, if there was a body stashed, someone would come out to check on it.

I put the spurs to Little Blackie, then, and covered as much ground as I could in the next hour. I didn't know whether to look for wagon tracks or just hoofprints, so I kept my eyes open for anything that might have come from the direction of the roadhouse. I tried to follow the irregularities in the land, as I hoped to find some nook or cranny where a bit of disturbed earth would not be very visible. To keep from being seen from far off, I kept to low ground whenever I could, which meant that I didn't always have good bearings.

I saw quite a few interesting things. In addition to bleached bones and dried-up carcasses, I saw a variety of cast-off items from people who had wandered here. I saw a knee-high woman's shoe that would have put a stout woman out of breath when she buttoned it. Its useful days had passed, though, as the leather had warped and the stitches had ruptured where the leather came across the big toe and joined the sole. I saw rusted cans, mangled bits of sheet iron, a coffeepot with a dozen bullet holes in it. A wagon wheel rim lay half buried in blown sand, and a mashed coal scuttle had a pile of rabbit pellets collected in a dented area. In the mouth of an old badger den, someone had taken the trouble of cramming a metal bracket that looked as if it had come off a wagon tongue.

Then I found a place where horses had come across the grassland in the recent past. How recent, I could not tell, as tracks on dry grass can last till snowfall. I followed them to a high spot, where I figured I was about a mile south-southwest from the inn. I turned around and followed the tracks the other way until I came to a gully with brush about four feet high. In among the brush, I could see footprints on fresh dirt.

I left there right away. I headed back to town, mapping out a plan. I was going to have to come at this in a roundabout way, and if anything went wrong with it, I was going to look awfully stupid. But compared with the way I felt when I woke up in the hag's room, feeling stupid would have been an improvement.

I rode straight for town on what I pictured as a diagonal, and I covered about two and a half miles. Then I turned back east and rode the horse at a walk until we got to the inn. I put him away in the stable, told Tim I didn't plan to leave that day, and went to my room. I looked through my bag and verified that my six-gun was still there, loaded as before. I hated to leave it behind, but I didn't want to raise any suspicion. So I put it away, locked the door behind me, and went up front. I found Mr. Gridley polishing a pair of cracked boots, which he had sitting on a newspaper on the seat of one of the dining room chairs.

I told him I would like to stay over for another night.

Without looking at me, he said, "Horse all right?"

"So-so. A day's rest won't hurt him, and I don't

feel like going anywhere. I felt queasy to my stomach even with the horse at a slow walk."

"Uh-huh."

I took out a silver dollar and laid it on the corner of the table. "Here's this," I said.

He tipped his head up. "Oh, fine."

"I need to go out and walk. Get my blood flowing, try to get some of this stuff worked out of me."

"Dinner should be in an hour or so."

"Don't wait for me," I said. "I don't know if I could hold it down anyway. I didn't do so well this morning."

"Sorry to hear that." He gave me a smile that I imagined was supposed to convey sympathy.

"Oh, I brought it on myself. I've got no complaint. I just need to get straightened out."

"Sure. You take care of yourself. If you want something to eat later on, just say so. We're always here." He smeared another gob of paste onto the boot he was working on, and I left him to that as I walked out into the daylight again.

I walked straight up to town and went into the general store, where I bought the sturdiest tin plate I could find. After that I walked to the edge of town, tucked the plate inside my shirt, and headed off on foot through the rolling country.

A little over an hour later, by my calculation, I found the gully. After taking a long look at the surrounding country, I scuttled down the slope and made my way into the bushes. There I found a broad area of tramped dirt, some of it with grass showing through. After kicking around for a moment, I figured someone had dug two holes and piled the loose dirt between them. I had a hunch I would find Grimes in one of the two depressions.

I stood facing the area with my back to the north, where the inn would be. Someone coming from that direction would probably have buried a body with its head to the south. And even if a person had no regard for human life, he would probably lay out two bodies the same way. That was the way I saw it, anyway, as I tried to put myself in the other person's position. As I nodded my head back and forth, I decided to try the left hole first. I took out the tin plate, got down on my knees, and started scraping dirt.

The work went slow, as I could move just a little dirt at a time. I started in the middle because I did not want to drag the edge of the plate across anyone's face. I scraped and scooped, and by the time I had dug out about a foot of dirt, the outline of a grave was very evident. I was tired and sweaty, and I had no water. My back ached because I had to reach down to haul out the dirt. But I knew I was better off than whoever was below me.

As I worked deeper into the hole, I had to get down in it to have any effectiveness. I scooped plateful after plateful of dirt, knowing as I did it that I was kneeling on somebody.

About two and a half feet down, the edge of the plate met some resistance—something that had a little give to it. I kept working in the middle, hoping I was crouched on the body's feet and not its face. I scraped and scooped for longer than I thought I would have to in order to uncover an arm. Then it rolled free—a coarse hand, a thick wrist, and the sleeve of a gray wool overshirt.

I let out a long breath. This was a hell of a thing to

be right about. I didn't think I had to dig any further in order to identify the body, but I did think I would want to look him over for wounds. First, though, I wanted to see who was in the other hole.

I went to work on it in the same way but taking a little less care at the beginning. From the position of the arm I figured Grimes was laid out with his head to the south, as I had thought. Assuming that the second body was laid out the same way and at about the same depth, I didn't feel that I had to be so tentative as I dug the first part.

All the time I was digging, I wondered whose body lay beneath my feet and hands. If it was Fernando, I would know him, even if some time had gone by since he was buried. If it was someone I didn't recognize, and if he looked as if he was cut from the same cloth as Grimes, I could guess he was Lawhorn the missing partner. Beyond that, I had no idea. It could be a woman. A child. A steamer trunk.

I was getting hungry now, and thirstier, but I had a job to do. Scrape, scoop, and toss. My feet and legs felt cramped. My wrists ached. I kept digging until I felt a familiar resistance. Then I scooped and brushed dirt with my hands until I uncovered an arm. I did not recognize it at first, so I scraped with the plate until I had the whole right arm in view. I brushed the dirt off the fabric, rubbed the sleeve of the coat between my thumb and my forefinger. Sackcloth. Not what I expected, but not a great surprise. Whoever had done this had no doubt taken the man's wallet of pictures.

I stood up and climbed out onto firm ground. I had found an odd pairing, all right. Now I had to look them over to see how they had come to this end. That meant more digging.

I needed a breather, and now that I wasn't so focused on finding out who was buried here, I began to think of the outer world. I walked to the nearest hilltop and looked around. The country looked broad and empty under an endless sky. Here I was, in the middle of nowhere, trying to make sense of two dead men. I remembered a saying I had heard once. Two men could keep a secret if one of them was dead. I wondered how many ways it worked in this arrangement.

Back down the hill I went to dig some more. I had to uncover Grimes all the way so that I could roll him over and look for holes. I found nothing, no evidence of a gunshot or a stab wound. I felt his head, and nothing seemed out of order there. I had already thought the Gridleys were capable of poisoning, and now it seemed like a strong possibility. They had Jeanette get me out of the way, and then they took care of Grimes. I remembered when Mr. Gridley went to the kitchen to ask for pie. It had all gone so smoothly that they must have had a system.

Now for the other body. I had the feeling that time was going to get away from me, so I worked fast. As I cleared away the dirt from the upper body, I thought I found bloodstains on the coat and shirt, but with the caking of dirt I couldn't be sure. So I pulled him up into a sitting position and inspected the rest of him. It didn't take much to see that Milaham had been stabbed in the back three times. As I thought about when I had seen him last, it occurred to me that he could have been done in at about the same time as Grimes, most likely in a different place as well as by a different method.

Re-burying the men did not take long. I pushed

piles of dirt with the plate, and I moved lesser amounts with the edge of my boot. When I was done, the whole area looked pretty close to the way it had looked when I first came upon it.

The sun was slipping as I walked back to town. I was going to have to make some account of having been away so long, and I was as dirty as a street urchin.

I left the tin plate beneath a clump of sagebrush at the edge of town and then walked to the main street. Lucky for me, the barber shop was open. I was able to wash up and get a shave, and I didn't have to answer a great many questions. I didn't know if I would fare as well when I got back to the Empire Inn.

CHAPTER NINE

I walked out of the barber shop feeling fresh and clean. A light motion of air played on my freshly shaven face and made me feel tender for a moment. But those feelings vanished as I turned to my right and saw that I was about ready to walk past the sheriff's office and the jail. Maybe it was superstition and maybe it was guilt, but I had a strong feeling that I didn't want to go that way. Although I knew I should report what I found, I was also afraid that doing it would throw everything into turmoil and disrupt my finding things out for my own purposes. The way I saw it, the two men I had found weren't going anywhere, so if I waited a day or two to report my finding, things would not change much. Meanwhile, I had to protect my chances of doing what I set out to do. One requirement, of course, was to keep myself alive, and I needed to think about how I was going to deal with the crew at the Empire Inn.

Rather than go past the sheriff's office, then, I went the other way, passed the corner, and crossed the main street to the saloon. I took note of its name this time—the Schooner—and walked on in.

The murky interior did not take me by surprise. As soon as my eyes adjusted I made out a bartender at the far end of the bar, which ran along the right wall. He was talking to two men who stood at the bar with their hats tipped back and their holstered six-guns on display. They were the only other people in the place. I remembered Chilo referring to ugly women who came in here, and I imagined they might show up a little later. Women like that usually went to work after dark, when the world was more hospitable to them.

I wasn't looking for women, though. My idea was to drink two quick glasses of beer so that I would have it on my breath when I went back to the inn. Then I could let on that I had spent a while here and a while at the barber shop.

I went to the bar and stood with my foot on the rail. The bartender, a short man with a big head and a round belly, came walking to my end. He asked what I wanted and poured me a glass of beer. I pushed a nickel toward him, and he picked it up without looking at me. Then he left me to myself as he went back to talk to the two range riders.

The first slug of beer tasted good. In addition to my usual reason for drinking it, I hoped it might relax my features. I looked at myself in the mirror and wondered how well I might pass for a simpleton when I got back to the inn. The shave helped. It gave me a clean, open expression. I needed to keep the innocent appearance, pick up anything I could without asking questions, and get out of the place in a casual way that would raise no suspicion.

I was convinced that the Gridleys were a pretty hardened bunch. If they could do in Grimes that easily, they had their methods well rehearsed, and they wouldn't let a pretended friendship with me get in the way.

Still, I didn't think that the blighted intentions of this locale were limited to the Gridleys. Grimes and Milaham's deaths were clearly related, but I had a hunch the Gridleys hadn't done the knife work. Although I could imagine Norma clutching a butcher knife in a murderous posture, the method did not match the calmer technique of lacing a piece of mince pie with arsenic. Furthermore, Milaham had told me he wouldn't have anything to do with that place. My guess was that someone across the way had done him in, probably to keep him from finding out something. His ending up in a grave next to Grimes suggested to me that the Gridleys were in cahoots with Mr. Frye. Maybe that was the connection. It seemed more probable than other speculations I had tried, such as Grimes and Milaham looking for the same person. Milaham wouldn't have been searching for Lawhorn any more than he would have been hunting for Fernando. And Grimes would not have been looking for Dr. McCabe's daughter, or anyone else in Milaham's wallet.

I nodded to myself. I would go with the Gridleys-and-Mr. Frye connection for right now. If I tried to force another one or tried to make the evidence fit a theory, I was setting myself up for failing to solve my problem, not to mention worse possibilities.

I finished my glass of beer and called for another. The short man with the large head and round belly served me as before, then left me to my thoughts.

I needed to be on my guard against Jeanette, along with everything else. Mama Spider. Whatever she put in my drink, I was not going to give her a chance to do it again. I felt like the fellow in the ancient story, Greek I think, who found out he'd eaten his own children. I felt I had taken in something tainted and I needed to get it out of my blood. That was the worst part. But I also felt that if I thought I deserved to get anywhere with Magdalena, I shouldn't be consorting with other women, especially of the harpy variety.

I still didn't have a definite plan as to what I was going to do the next day. If I went much further at all in trying to dig up information, I would have to tip my hand in some way. That meant I had to get clear of the Empire Inn first. After that, I could get back on track in my search for Fernando, asking questions and keeping a weather eye out.

The door opened, and I saw a crack of daylight over my right shoulder. I looked ahead in the mirror as the door closed off the light and a man moved toward the bar in an uneven gait. I looked directly at him and recognized the stoop-shouldered form. Then I turned my gaze to the mirror again and picked out the battered hat, the narrow chin, and the thatch of hair.

The bartender came halfway down the bar to the place where Tim the stable man stood. After a low exchange, the bartender poured a shot glass of whiskey. Tim laid a coin on the bar, poured the liquor down the hatch, and turned and left. Daylight showed and then disappeared. I went back to my thoughts and my beer.

The second one went down almost as fast as the first, and reminding myself that I didn't need any more, I walked out into the early evening. It was a little later than it had been the day before when I took my stroll, but the sun had not yet gone down. The shadows were lengthening, and the town had a different tone to it—very much the way a canyon or a gully will take on a different cast from one time of day to another. When I came to the cross street, I looked to my left to see if I could catch any movement at the house where I had seen Milaham talking to the bent-over man. I saw no one, and the house looked dark.

I walked on, feeling detached from this little world of Raven Springs. I felt washed out from my day's work, hungry from not having had anything to eat since morning, light-headed and relaxed from the two glasses of beer I had just put down, and puzzled by the knowledge that people could disappear in one or both of the roadside inns and the rest of the town seemed to take no notice at all. The barber went on shaving, the bartender went on pouring drinks, and the merchant went on weighing out beans. For all I knew, every business on this little main street was a front for a torture chamber, an opium den, or a sodomy parlor.

Back to earth, Jimmy, I told myself. Not everybody in the world was as treacherous as Mr. Gridley, who could have a paying guest killed and buried overnight, then go about polishing a pair of boots as if he had done nothing more serious than empty a mousetrap.

Gridley and Grimes. I wondered who could have imagined I would end up in a web like this when I set out to find Fernando and the Virgin. But it made sense, I told myself. If I was going to look for someone who disappeared, I shouldn't be surprised to end up in a place where other people dropped out of sight as well. Finding Milaham buried next to Grimes suggested to me that this had been the edge of the world where a range of people had dropped off.

I wanted to think that hovering above this place, like an eagle, was a God's-eye knowledge and conscience, some power that would make sure the truth came out and people got punished. But I knew it was possible that some people could simply vanish and no one would know to come here to try to account for them. Life went on, disappearances went unsolved, the perpetrators picked up and went someplace else. Some malefactors got caught, and others went on clucking their tongues and polishing boots.

One thing at a time, I reminded myself. I'd better keep my eye on the main task. Then if I could do something for the greater good, so much the better.

As I walked past the general store, I thought of buying some provisions, but I decided it might show too much caution if I arrived at the inn with my own vittles. Then I wavered. I was hungry, and if things didn't look right at the dining table, I ran the chance of not getting anything to eat until the next day. So I went in and bought two good-sized sticks of jerky. I put one in my pocket, and as I stepped down from the sidewalk I bit into the other.

I sauntered down the main street, enjoying the

taste of the dried beef, salt, and pepper. I was trying to imagine how things might shape up at the Gridley table, when I thought I heard whistling behind me. It was a continuous sound, lasting five seconds at a stretch, not unlike a steam whistle but not so loud and shrill. After I heard it three or four times, I turned to look, and there in the middle of the street came Chilo poking along on his mule.

I took another bite of jerky as I waited for him to catch up. He had a broad smile on his face, and I imagined he was glad to see someone he could talk to in his own language.

"Hello, Chilo," I said. "How goes it?"

"Just here, is all. And you?"

"Taking a walk. Wondering where the girls are."

He threw back his head and laughed.

"I looked in the cantina, and I didn't see even the ugly ones."

He laughed again. "They come out after dark."

"And you, you get back before dark, so *la llorona* doesn't get you?"

"Oh, that's for little children."

"I thought I saw her. The old maid sister."

He kept his mouth closed on a smile as he shook his head.

"Maybe she's not *la llorona*," I said. "I think she kidnaps sailors."

He gave a small laugh now, which seemed to be his way of countering anything he wasn't sure of. "Maybe so."

I paused for a moment, and he waited for me to speak. Then I said, "There's another person in this town who strikes me as curious."

A look of amusement played on his face.

"An old man, fat and bent over. He leans on a stick, like a cane. He lives back there, around the corner."

"Oh, yes. Bruno."

"Does he know a great deal?"

"He is very nosy. He always has much gossip."

"Really? About what?"

"About everybody in the town. He talks to everyone who passes by his house."

"Does he know about travelers?"

"I don't know. He hardly leaves his house. Just to go to the store."

"Does he buy candy?"

The small laugh. "I don't know. They carry his food home for him."

"That's good." I held another pause. "I'll tell you, I'd like to know about a man who might have come through here about a month ago."

"You could ask with the people at the inn."

"I've already asked them all the questions I can. Does Bruno talk a lot, or is he a person of confidence?"

"Oh, he tells everything to everybody he knows."

"That is to say, if someone asks him some questions, he might tell someone else about it."

"Maybe."

"But you, you're not like that, are you?"

He smiled. "I don't know."

"Well, I want to ask about a man, but I don't want everyone to know I'm asking." I took out my other piece of jerky and handed it to him. "You understand."

He thanked me and bit off a piece.

I shrugged. "It's hard to know who is of confidence. But I think you are."

"Maybe."

"More than Bruno."

He tossed back his head and laughed.

"Here it is. I'm looking for a man who came this way about a month ago. A Mexican. Very decent, well-dressed. Clean. Very serious and reserved. He would have been carrying a bulky package."

"Tall? Short?"

"Tall. And traveling by himself."

After some hesitation, Chilo said, "I think I saw him."

"Really? Did he stay here?"

I don't think so. He passed by here in the afternoon, and he followed the road to Rawlins."

"And he had a bundle?"

"It looked like a small sack of grain."

"It might have been a grain sack. And you say he went on to Rawlins?"

"That's what it looked like."

"You didn't talk to him?"

"No. Like you say, he was serious. He didn't seem interested in talking with other people."

I was starting to get excited at this little bit of knowledge, but again I didn't want to force the details to match what I wanted to hear. And even if Chilo had seen Fernando, the possibility remained that he didn't make it to Rawlins. I decided to go back to the scenario in which Fernando made it as far as Raven Springs but no further. I knew that was what happened to Grimes, and I thought it might have happened to his partner, Lawhorn, so it was a good possibility for Fernando as well. In any of those circumstances, somebody had to have a way of getting rid of the goods and horses.

"Tell me something else," I said. "Who buys and sells mules and horses?'

He shrugged. "Various people."

"No, I mean, who buys and sells them for a business? Does somebody come through here to buy extra animals, or does a person have to take them somewhere?"

"Oh, there comes a man who buys them."

"Very good. And who does he buy them from?"

"Whoever has anything to sell."

"I understand, but is there someone who sells more than others?"

"I don't know."

"That's all right. Do you know where this man comes from?"

"Rolens."

"Rawlins?"

"Yes. Somewhere in that direction." Chilo waved toward the north.

I nodded. "And his name? Do you know what he is called?"

"Eslón."

"Sloan?"

"Yes. Eslón."

I looked to the north. "If the man I'm looking for went that way, and if the man who buys extra horses lies there, maybe I should go and see what I can find out."

"Do you want to buy a horse, or sell one?"

"Neither one, precisely. But I would like to talk to someone who buys them. So if I go there, I will try to find him." Then, as a courtesy, I said, "Do you want to go?"

Chilo laughed, leaning back. "I have to work."

"For Franklin."

"Yes."

"Are there girls there, in Rawlins?"

He laughed. "I don't know. One or another. There are more things in Rolens than here. This town doesn't have anything."

"If I find a pretty one, and if I see you again, I'll tell you where she is."

"You come back through here?"

"Probably. I have to leave first, of course. Is there anything you'd like from Rawlins?"

He shook his head.

I winked at him. "Maybe I'll see you later, then, Chilo."

"That's fine."

"If I do, I'll tell you if I see any pretty ones. But I think you already know, and you won't tell me."

He gave a clever smile now. "Very far away. Very far."

I walked into the front part of the inn to find all the family members eating beef stew. A large crockery dish sat in the middle of the table, with a metal spoon sticking out of it. Mr. Gridley turned in his seat and smiled as he looked me up and down.

"Well, hello, young fella. I thought maybe we'd lost ya."

"Not yet. I just got sidetracked in a couple of places."

"Oh?"

"I thought maybe I'd get a shave, and I had to wait a while for that. And then time got away from me in a place called the Schooner."

"That can happen."

"It sure can. The first couple I drank knocked the edge off of how ragged I felt from last night, and then after that, why, everything smoothed out."

"We didn't know if you'd be back for supper, so we went ahead and got started."

"Good enough."

"Pull up a chair and join us."

The lodgers' side of the table was unoccupied, so I took a seat where Grimes had sat the night before. At the same time, Norma got up and went into the kitchen. I looked down the table and gave a blank nod to Jeanette and the children, then set my hat on the chair next to me. Norma came through the door and handed me a bowl and a spoon, then sat down. I noticed the head scarf, tied under the chin with the two loose ends hanging down. No one seemed to be paying me any attention in particular, and the meal went on with the usual sounds of spoons clacking and people eating. I served myself a bowl of stew and dug in.

Mr. Gridley's voice came up from about a yard away and made me flinch. "Well, what did you learn today?"

"Not much."

"Little town like this always has gossip, if you hang out in barber shops and saloons."

"I suppose so, but I don't ask many questions. I'm just not naturally curious."

"Neither am I," said the host. "Doesn't seem like a bad way to be."

"Of course, you hear things whether you ask or not."

"Is that right?" He rested his spoon in the bowl and looked at me.

"Oh, yeh," I answered. "Jokes an' such. Things you can't remember when you want to, and other things you can't forget. Poems an' ditties."

"There's never any shortage of that sort of thing." Mr. Gridley gave a benevolent smile.

"I should say. There was this one I heard in there today, maybe you've heard it. But I can't get it out of my head." I looked at the children. "Don't listen too close." Then I gave a gallant smile to Norma and recited:

> "Oh, Daisy, Daisy,
> Give me your answer do,
> For I'm half crazy,
> All for the love of you.
> It won't be a stylish marriage,
> As I can't afford a carriage,
> But you'll look sweet
> Upon the seat
> Of a bicycle built for two.
>
> "Oh, Bill, oh, Bill,
> Here is your answer true.
> Oh, Bill, oh, Bill,
> I don't know what we can do.
> For we can't have a marriage
> Without a carriage,
> And I'll be damned
> If I'll be crammed
> On a bicycle built for two."

Mr. Gridley produced a little "heh, heh, heh," and nobody else said anything.

I looked at my bowl and shrugged. "I'm afraid

GET 4 FREE BOOKS!

You can have the best Westerns delivered to your door for less than what you'd pay in a bookstore or online. Sign up for one of our book clubs today, and we'll send you 4 FREE* BOOKS, worth $23.96, just for trying it out...with no obligation to buy, ever!

Authors include classic writers such as
LOUIS L'AMOUR, MAX BRAND, ZANE GREY
and more; PLUS new authors such as
COTTON SMITH, TIM CHAMPLIN, JOHNNY D. BOGGS
and others.

As a book club member you also receive the following special benefits:
- 30% OFF all orders through our website & telecenter!
- Exclusive access to special discounts!
- Convenient home delivery and 10 days to return any books you don't want to keep.

There is no minimum number of books to buy, and you may cancel membership at any time. See back to sign up!

*Please include $2.00 for shipping and handling.

YES! ☐

Sign me up for the Leisure Western Book Club and send my FOUR FREE BOOKS! If I choose to stay in the club, I will pay only $14.00* each month, a savings of $9.96!

NAME: _____

ADDRESS: _____

_____

TELEPHONE: _____

E-MAIL: _____

☐ **I WANT TO PAY BY CREDIT CARD.**

☐ VISA   ☐ MasterCard.   ☐ DISCOVER

ACCOUNT #: _____

EXPIRATION DATE: _____

SIGNATURE: _____

Send this card along with $2.00 shipping & handling to:

**Leisure Western Book Club
1 Mechanic Street
Norwalk, CT 06850-3431**

Or fax (must include credit card information!) to: 610.995.9274.
You can also sign up online at www.dorchesterpub.com.

JOIN NOW!

that's the best I can do for today. I'm not much of a traveling minstrel."

"Quite all right," said the host. "Not everyone has to be." After a few seconds of silence, he spoke again. "So, are you expectin' to move on in the mornin'?"

I looked up, and all three adults seemed to be giving me a narrow gaze. "Oh, yeh. I've laid over long enough." Then I added, "Couldn't ask for a better place, though."

Mr. Gridley sat up straight and poked at his lower teeth with a toothpick. "Hope the good weather holds out."

As soon as I finished my bowl of stew, I said I was tired and went to my room. By lamplight I checked my belongings again and found everything the same as before. Then, doing my best to be quiet, I moved the metal bedstead an inch at a time until I had it lodged against the door. With my pillow at the other end, and with my six-gun on the chair a foot away, I blew out the lamp and went to bed.

Gray morning light was filtering into the room when I awoke. I was surprised not to have heard anything in the night, and in a small, odd way, I was surprised to still be alive. I lay in bed for a few minutes to let the world fill in around me, and then I put my feet on the floor and got started on the day.

I dressed, pulled on my boots, and put my bag in order. Inch by inch, with as quiet movements as I could manage, I put the bed back in its original position. After taking a final look around, I put on my hat and tiptoed out of the room. I paused for a moment in the hallway, wavering, and decided to go out the back door. I turned left, walked past a couple of rooms on either side, and stepped out into the morning.

The air was crisp, so I set down my bag, took out my coat, and put it on. As I did so, I thought once again that I would like to have my pistol on me, but I reminded myself that I didn't want to stir up any suspicion. I closed the bag and headed for the stable, clearing my throat and then rapping once on the wood before I opened the door.

Tim was standing inside, between the grain box and the pile of hay. He was leaning on his pitchfork and smoking a cigarette.

"Good mornin'," I said.

He squinted and nodded as he took a drag on his quirly.

"I think I'll go ahead and get my horse," I said.

"I just fed 'em."

I looked over and saw a bay horse in the stall next to Blackie. Both of them were chomping away. I thought it should be customary to feed the horses earlier, so they would be ready for anyone who wanted to get a good start on the day, but I said nothing. I glanced at my saddle and my horse. Everything seemed in order.

"I'll be back in a little bit," I said, and I walked out. I went around to the front of the inn, as if by habit, and I found the door locked. As I was walking back down the steps, I heard the latch and then the opening of the door. I turned around to see Mr. Gridley looking out at me.

"Oh, it's you," he said, giving me a close look. "Have you been out?"

"I just went to check on my horse. I went out the back door but I didn't think to come in the same way."

His face relaxed. "No harm in that. Come on in." He stood aside.

I stepped up onto the porch. "I just came to give you the key," I said, handing it forward with my left hand as I walked toward him.

"Come in and have breakfast."

I stopped at the doorway, scrunching my nose and upper lip in a way that I hoped would look stupid. "Thanks all the same, but I didn't do much yesterday to get an appetite. And my stomach still feels queasy."

"Have some coffee at least."

I gave a pained look now. "I don't think it would set well. But thanks." I held the key forward again, and he took it.

"Good enough. Are you on your way, then?"

"As soon as I get my horse saddled." I shifted the bag to my left hand and touched my hatbrim. "I want to thank you for your hospitality."

He gave me his benevolent smile. "Our thanks to you. And whenever you come through this way again, stop in."

"I'll be sure to." I heard footsteps from within, like boot heels on a wood floor, and then a man's voice.

Mr. Gridley spoke over his shoulder. "I'll be right there." Then he turned to me and said, "So long, Jimmy. Good luck in your work."

"Thanks." I heard the door close behind me as I walked to the steps.

Out in the stable, Tim stood by loitering as I went

about my work. I took my time saddling the horse and tying my bag onto the back. I imagined my fellow traveler was having breakfast and making small talk with the landlord. I wouldn't have minded getting a look at him, and if I had given any more thought to seeing the second horse, I might have gone in for a cup of coffee, but I had stuck to my plan of caution. Now it was just something to think about.

I felt Tim's eyes on me, and I glanced his way to see him look down at a rope splice he was twisting and pushing on. Finally I pulled the horse's head out of the stanchion, put the bridle on him, and led him out of the stall.

"So long," I said to Tim. "See you next time."

He said something like "Yum" as I took the horse past him.

Outside in the cool morning, I led Little Blackie onto the road and walked with him. I studied the Falconer House and wished I could think of some excuse for going in. Even if I could think of one, it was still early in the day. I walked the horse a quarter of a mile, then stopped him to check things over. I pulled out my rifle and could not see where anyone had tampered with it. My bedroll and saddle bags looked the same as before, also. I walked Little Blackie the rest of the short way into town.

Things were just beginning to stir on the main street. The door of the general store was open, and ringing blows sounded from the blacksmith shop across the way. The smell of woodsmoke hung on the air, and I thought of my fellow lodger eating my share of the flapjacks. All the same, I didn't mind having missed the chance.

When I came to the cross street where I had seen Milaham talking to the old man, I paused on the other side and gazed back. The house looked as dark as the evening before, and I was about to move on when a slight sound carried on the morning air and a movement in the back yard caught my eye. The outhouse door opened, and the stooped old man came hobbling out. He was dressed for the day, complete with his short-billed cap, laborer's shirt, suspenders, and loose trousers.

I angled across the street and stopped in his front yard. I whistled once, twice.

The old man came around the corner of the house, slow and halting, bent over and leaning on his stick. I waved. He lifted his head like an ancient bulldog, then lowered it and came forward. When he was within fifteen feet of me, he spoke.

"Whatty you want?"

"Are you Mr. Bruno?"

"Bruno. Just-a Bruno."

"Good enough."

"You want sawm thing? I not gonna stand out here all mornin'."

"I thought I would ask you about somebody."

"I don't know nawthing." He lifted his head and moved it around. "Ask anny boddy. I'm a stupid old man. I don't know nawthing."

"Someone told me you know a lot."

He raised his free hand and beckoned to me. "Cawm over here."

I walked up to within four feet of him, with my horse standing in back of me. I could see his bristly white hair and week-long whiskers, his bleary eyes, the purple edges on his nostrils. I caught a whiff of his old-man smell. Then I saw yellow stumps of teeth as he spoke.

"Every boddy wants to know sawm thing. Just like you. But I don' know you."

"My name's Jimmy Clevis. I saw you talking to a man the day before yesterday. I know him. We know some of the same people."

Bruno looked me up and down. "You wanna know what he wanna know?"

"Not necessarily. Maybe about someone else."

He waved his hand around next to his head. "Not today. You cawm back when I'm not so busy."

"Later today?"

He raised his voice and said, "I tahl you, not to-day. Maybe sawm awther day." He shifted his weight as he leaned forward on his stick.

"Were you a butcher?" I asked.

He looked straight at me. "I wass a baker. But no boddy cares. That wass long time a-go."

I had had a hard time earlier trying to imagine him putting a knife into Milaham's back, and it seemed even less probable now. "Good enough, Bruno. I won't bother you any more today. Glad to meet you, and maybe I'll see you some other day."

"Yah, yah. You all the same." He turned and moved away.

I walked back out onto the main street and stood for a moment next to the little black horse. The day was just beginning, and already I had run out of things to do in this town. I had gotten out of the Empire Inn all right, and I was glad of that, but I still needed to be cautious about tipping my hand. I wished for all I was worth that I could get into the Falconer House before I left town, but I couldn't think of a way. That would have to wait until I came back.

I had decided that much, at least. I would come through here again, regardless of what I found else-where. I didn't like riding away and not doing any-thing about Grimes, but a voice inside me told me that if I blew the top off of that keg right now, it would keep me from finding Fernando. My gut feel-ing was that he hadn't made it any farther than this town, but I had to follow the other two leads I had gotten from Chilo. In addition to that, I had to go to the sheep camp where Fernando had been headed. I knew where to find Grimes whenever I came back, which I didn't think would be very long, and I could call up that part of the investigation whenever it seemed best.

The way I saw it, Grimes and I were pals, if only for a short while. He didn't play his part very well, but he still didn't deserve what he got. I had an obli-gation to bring his killers to justice, and I had more than a hunch as to who they were. But I wanted to make them answer for as much as I could get on them, and it would take me a little while to deter-mine whether Fernando might be part of it. After that, I would be back.

I swung into the saddle and gathered my reins. As I put my spurs to the little black horse, I thought of Bruno tapping the ground with his stick. Some other day.

CHAPTER TEN

Out on the trail away from Raven Springs, I began to think again about the breakfast I had paid for and not eaten. As things turned out, I could probably have put on the feed bag just as I had done the morning before. It was a small sacrifice, I told myself. I had gotten clear of the place. Now all I had to do was find out where I was going to get something to eat today.

About two hours into my ride, I saw what looked like a road ranch or way station of sorts. It consisted of a low-slung main building with a couple of mismatched sheds in back. It looked like a place where a fellow might be able to get a meal and maybe some information.

A man with dark red hair, a splotchy pink-and-white complexion, and a cook's belly welcomed me in. I asked him if he served food, and he said he sure did. He could fix me up a plate of steak and spuds in two shakes. I said fine and took a seat at one of the three tables in the middle of his little establishment.

On the two sides, the walls were cluttered with hanging goods for sale—rat traps, leather thongs, rolled canvas, ax handles, odd lengths of chain, and such. Along the back wall the proprietor had shelves of provisions, and in the left corner sat a wood cookstove, where he chucked in a few lengths of firewood about an inch thick. He went into a store room and came back with a hunk of meat, which he flopped onto a little counter near the stove. Then he produced a square-headed mace, the likes of which I had seen before, and he took to beating the steak. After about fifteen blows he turned the steak over and pounded it again. Next he held his open hand above the top of the cookstove for about five seconds and put an iron skillet on the stove top. From a tin can he spooned two gobs of bacon grease, then shook the skillet and tipped it one way and another. He looked at me and smiled.

"Comin' right along."

"Mighty fine," I said.

He went into the back room again and came out with two potatoes. After rubbing them one at a time with a cloth he had hanging from his belt, he sliced the spuds with a foot-long knife that looked as if it had been used for everything from cutting forage to splitting kindling. Thick black smoke was coming off the skillet, and the grease made a loud sputtering sound when he laid the steak in it. He slid the potato slices in on each side of the meat, poked at them with the knife, and salted the whole mess.

"Just a couple minutes now," he said, raising his eyebrows and smiling again.

"Good." I folded my hands over my stomach and made myself be patient. I could smell the grease, and a moment later I could smell the frying beef. Things were shaping up fine, and I was hungry.

"Where you headed?" he asked.

"Towards Rawlins."

"Looks like you've got good weather for it."

"I hope so."

He screwed up his mouth for a minute and poked again at the grub in the skillet. "I'm sorry I don't have any coffee," he said. "I run out of it, and I won't get any more for a couple of days."

"That's the one thing I've got left," I said. "I was campin' on the first part of my trip, and I came out even on everything except coffee."

"Well, if you want to bring it in, I'll boil us up some."

"Sure." I got up and headed for the door. As soon as I had my back to him, it occurred to me that I was giving him a chance to put something in my food. Then I realized he could have the same fear about me if he wanted. I went out to my horse, dug around and found the little bag of coffee, and brought it in.

The red-haired man was putting an open pan of water on the stove top. "Good boy," he said as I handed him the bag. He reached under the counter and came out with a spatula that looked like a cousin to his battered knife. He flipped the steak and the potato slices and then stood back.

"Sumbitch gets hot."

"I bet." I stood next to my chair, admiring the browned grub in the skillet.

He stepped forward again, salted the food, and moved back.

"My name's Jimmy Clevis," I said. "I'm glad I stopped. That food is startin' to smell pretty good."

"It sure is." He transferred the spatula to his left hand and reached over to shake mine. "Del Scoggin," he said. "Glad you stopped in."

I took my seat. "Many travelers come by this way?" I asked.

"A few. Sometimes more than others."

I waited half a minute and then said, "I was wonderin' if you might have seen a fella I'm on the lookout for."

"Hard to say. I don't see 'em all."

"This would have been a Mexican fella, taller than average, always clean in his appearance. Would have come through here about a month ago."

"What kind of a horse did he ride?"

"A sorrel, from what I understood."

The man shook his head. "Sure doesn't sound familiar."

"A friend of some friends," I said. "Came up this way from Colorado, and then no one heard from him."

Scoggin tipped his head and turned it, as if to say, "What do you think of that?"

"I met a fellow in Raven Springs who said he thought he might have seen my man come through. Then he mentioned a man from Rawlins that I thought I might look up if I could find him."

"Oh?"

"A fella named Sloan. Probably comes through this way."

"The horse trader?'

"That's the one, I believe."

"Him I know. He does come through here. I can't say I see him every time, though."

"I'm not too particular about when he came

through, but I'd like to know how to find him, just to ask him a few questions."

Scoggin tipped his head again. "I don't think he's that hard to find. I believe he's got a set of corrals on the road goin' out of Rawlins toward Medicine Bow."

"I see. Do you think there's anything about him that I should know?"

The man smiled and showed a set of yellow teeth. "Nothin' I could say with any certainty. He's a horse trader."

"Sure," I said. "He's not my main order of business anyway."

"The Mexican fella is."

"That's right. This one man said he thought he saw someone by that description go through Raven Springs, but I've got my doubts, because he didn't end up where he was supposed to go after that. I wish I'd thought to ask about the horse."

"You think it might have been someone else he saw?"

"I don't know. The man I'm trying to find was carrying a bundle. He had a figurine of the Virgin wrapped up in it, and he was supposed to take it to a sheep camp. This fella in Raven Springs, I told him about the bundle, but I forgot to mention the horse."

The proprietor screwed up his mouth again. "I tell ya, it could've been someone else. There's a fella from Rawlins that comes through here every once in a while. He's a pretty clean, tight customer. He looks a little like a Mexican, but he isn't one."

"Ah-hah. What's his name?"

"Contreras. He's got a business in Rawlins."

"Do you know if he came through here about a month ago?"

"I think that might have been when it was. I didn't think of him until you mentioned a bundle."

"Oh, really?"

"He was riding a big, dark horse, and he had what looked like a sack of grain tied across the back of his saddle. It wasn't a big item, maybe thirty or forty pounds. When it comes in a smaller weight like that, you might think it's rolled oats or something."

"A burlap bag, then?"

"That's right. Tight little package. And I think a man would have to be pretty reckless to try to take a peek in it."

"Is this fellow Contreras dangerous?"

The red-haired man raised his eyebrows. "From what I understand, he deals in gems. And I don't think it would be easy to come up behind him, much less lighten his load."

"Do you think I could find him at his business there in Rawlins?"

"You might, but if you go looking for him, you'd better go through the front door."

"That's advice I've heard before. A fellow gets in less trouble if he can remember to follow it."

"I'd say so." Scoggin moved forward and poked at the food in the skillet. "Just about ready," he said.

Back on the road after about an hour at Scoggin's roadhouse, I felt good—warm and full as a pup with meat, potatoes, and coffee. I didn't expect my next two stops to be so hospitable.

As I rode into Rawlins in the early afternoon, I formed an impression of it as being a wind-blown, dust-bitten town, not softened at all by the railroad. I knew it had begun as an end-of-track town, and af-

ter a rugged start it had acquired a legacy of string-
ing up undesirables who went too far in the line of
stealing horses, robbing trains, and breaking jail.
But the country around it offered good grazing for
sheep and cattle, so not everyone was likely to be a
desperado or a vigilante.

After asking in a couple of places for Sloan's corral, I found myself on the east side of town. As the
second person had assured me, I couldn't miss it.
The main building looked like an old way station,
being built of sod with only one door in front and no
windows. The corrals reached back behind it in an
uneven sprawl. It was evident that they had been
added on over a period of time, patched and rigged
with whatever the current owner had on hand.
Planks and poles with sometimes a tree branch,
brought from who knows where, were spliced with
rawhide and broken ropes, with here and there a
length of barbed wire running through. A speckled
horse in a near corral gave a whinny and came running up to the rail to look at Blackie and me.

The heavy wooden door in the front of the building opened, and a man appeared. I swung down
and walked forward a few steps.

"Good afternoon," I said.

He nodded and muttered something I didn't catch.

"Are you Mr. Sloan?"

"All day."

"Well, my name's Jimmy Clevis, sir, and they told
me I might be able to find you here."

He stepped into the daylight, and as his gaze slid
past me to take in my horse, I got a look at him. He
was an average-sized man, a little past his prime,
though I don't know how fine a figure he might

have cut at his best. He stood on spindly legs that had the job of holding up a poochy belly, and his narrow shoulders sagged. Beneath a short-brimmed hat he had straight, mouse-colored hair. He hadn't shaved in a few days, and the stubble did not flatter his slack cheeks and receding chin. His mouth opened in a kind of rectangle as he looked over my horse, and I saw a set of narrow, yellow teeth. He had pale brown eyes, and their whites were yellow, also. His glance came back to me.

"Buyin' or sellin'?"

"Neither one, at the moment. I'm mainly lookin' for information."

"I've never had much of that."

"It always seems to be scarce," I said. "I've been lookin' for a man who disappeared."

"Friend of yours?"

"Sort of. A friend of some friends. They asked me to see if I could find out what might have become of him."

Sloan's gaze relaxed, and it drifted to Little Blackie again.

"I think he made it as far as Raven Springs, but after that I don't know."

The man shrugged.

"I understood that you make it down that way."

"Not much."

"You might remember this fellow. He's a Mexican, taller than most, always clean and well-groomed."

Sloan shook his head. "I don't keep much of a lookout for them, except for around my own stock, of course."

"This would have been about a month ago."

He closed his eyes as he shook his head again.

"Did you happen to buy any horses down that way, along about then?"

His eyes were slits. "Not at all. I just about never go there. I stay busy right here. Most of my business comes to me."

"Do you know of anyone who sells horses there?"

"Not to mention."

"Do you know a man named Cale Gridley?"

He opened his eyes and held them full on me. "You've got a lot of questions, mister. I'll tell you who sells horses. People as has 'em, that's who. Same with the ones that buys 'em. Today it's one person, tomorrow it's another. That's business."

I decided to give it one more try. "This fellow I'm lookin' for would have been riding a sorrel horse."

"So would've a thousand other men. It's like sayin' he was wearin' a hat." Sloan took out a jack-knife, much cleaner and newer than I would have expected him to have, and started working on the fingernails of his left hand. I noticed that the fingers of both hands were yellowed.

"I suppose so. But I don't think you can blame me for asking."

His eyes met mine again. "Not for a minute."

I took leave of him then, and thanked him for his trouble, which he said was none at all. I walked my horse out a few yards, and as I mounted up, I saw that Sloan had put away his knife and was building himself a cigarette. For a fellow who didn't look any more hard-shelled than a peanut, he did all right for himself.

With only one inquiry I was able to find the business location of Frank Contreras, a block off of the main street. The lettering on his window confirmed what Scoggin had told me, that he was a dealer of gems. A bell tinkled as I opened the door into a room about fifteen feet square. Through a doorway in the back of the room I could see a black vault with a chromium handle and gilt letters. Then a man appeared from somewhere in the back room, and he came through the doorway.

From my conversation with Scoggin I was prepared to meet a tough man, and my first impression did not disappoint me. He looked as hard to crack as a black walnut.

He was dressed in a jacket and a vest, with the poise of a man who has a gun in a shoulder holster. Tall and broad-chested, he had dark hair, combed up and back in a neat fit. He had a narrow mustache as well, along with dark eyes and a tan complexion that had a sheen to it. The eyebrows grew close together, and his eyes had a narrow cast to them as he looked down at me from behind his glass counter.

"Yes, sir," he said.

"Are you Mr. Contreras?"

"Yes, I am."

"My name's Jimmy Clevis, and I'm traveling through."

He lowered his eyelids and nodded.

"I'm looking for a man who disappeared."

He pushed up his lip and mustache. "Men do that."

"Yes, and his friends, who are my friends as well, asked me if I could find out anything about him."

"And someone led you to think that I might be able to help you?"

"Not exactly. I made that assumption myself."

"Indeed."

"If you don't mind, I can give you a quick summary."

"Quick is best." The eyebrows flicked, and he seemed to look past me for a second.

"Well, the man I'm trying to find, or find out about, came from Colorado up this way. He was going to a sheep camp, where he was supposed to deliver a figurine of the Virgin. I think I tracked him as far as Raven Springs, and then after that I'm not sure. One man I talked to said he saw someone by that description go through the town."

"By what description?"

"The man's name is Fernando Molina Valdés. As you might guess by the name, he's Mexican. A tall man, by their standards at least, and a neat, clean dresser. He would have been carrying the Virgin wrapped up in a bundle."

Contreras was making a matter-of-fact expression with the side of his mouth. "And someone thought he saw him."

"Yes. But then I talked to someone else, who said you might have ridden through there at about that time."

"Which would have been?"

"About a month ago."

"I make business trips from time to time. On occasion I go through there."

"If you don't mind my asking, did you go through Raven Springs about a month ago?"

"What would it matter?"

"My thought is that Molina Valdés might not have made it any farther than Raven Springs, and that there might be a case of mistaken identity here."

He seemed to stiffen. "I see. Do you think I look like your friend Mr. Valdés?"

"Not really. But in a general way, someone might, shall I say, mismatch the description."

"What did you say your name is?"

"Clevis. Jimmy Clevis."

"Very well, Mr. Clevis. Let me tell you something. I am of Spanish descent. I am not Mexican. If someone takes me for a Mexican, I do not find it very flattering, much less intelligent."

"I hope you understand, it's someone else's impressions that I'm trying to clear up."

"Not very good ones, I'd say."

"And the reason I'm troubling you is to confirm that the other observation, that you yourself went through there at about that time, has some basis."

"I have my reasons for going where I go, and I don't feel that I have to answer any questions about my movements, either before or after the fact."

"I appreciate your discretion," I said. "And the opportunity for the conversation." I thought he would expect me to start to leave, but I didn't budge. "By the way, have you ever stayed at either of the two lodging houses as you come into Raven Springs from the east?"

He smiled without opening his mouth. "I've never had the pleasure."

"Have you ever known a man named Milaham?"

A thoughtful expression crossed his face, and he shook his head. "Nor that one either."

I thanked him for his time, and as I walked out the door I felt his eyes on me. He didn't like people prying, I could tell that, but I had come and gone through the front door, and as far as my business went, I didn't think he had a thing to lie about. I couldn't say the same for the other nut I had tried to crack in Rawlins.

As I had been given to understand from the beginning, the ranch where Fernando had been headed lay west and south of Rawlins. On the basis of Chanate's pronunciation, which came out something like Prestone, I imagined the ranch's name was Preston. I confirmed that name easily enough before I left Rawlins, then traveled with the afternoon sun in my eyes most of the way. I rode into the ranch itself in the early evening. A couple of dogs came out barking, and then an old man appeared at the bunkhouse door. He sent me another ten miles west, so darkness was beginning to draw in when I arrived at the sheep camp.

It smelled like sheep and looked like other such camps I had seen—low, drab buildings huddled next to a network of pens. A squalid-looking sod house had a light showing through a window, so I knocked on the door.

I heard voices, and the door opened to show me one man and then another standing in back of them. They looked like brothers, neither of them very big and both of them going gray. I spoke to them in Spanish, identifying myself and telling them what my errand was, and they invited me in.

I sat at a table in the middle of the one-room shanty. Overhead, a kerosene lamp sent out light that didn't quite reach the edges and corners of the room. One man, who introduced himself as Alfonso, sat down across from me while the other, Enrique, stirred a pot that sent forth the odors of mutton stew.

Alfonso had his two bottom front teeth missing, which flattened out some of his pronunciation, but I understood him well enough. He was friendly and outgoing. He told me they called their sheep camp "La Capilla," or the Chapel. He pointed out an alcove against one wall, where a cross hung above an altar-like shelf that held an array of different-sized candles. They had planned to put the Virgin there, but only God knew what had become of Fernando. They named the camp after a ranch in their home country, he explained. It was near a ranch called La Reforma and another called Los Sauces. This was a good ranch, very cold in the winter, but the owner, señor Preston, was a good boss. He kept them supplied with whatever they needed, and he gave them time every winter to go see their families.

Enrique spoke up from his place at the stove. They never lacked for food, he said, but he wished the *patrón* would bring them a different kind of meat. He hoped I liked *borrego*, which I understood to mean lamb or mutton either one.

It was fine, I said.

Alfonso said they were going to kill a young one in a couple of days and cook it on a spit, *a la vuelta y vuelta.* He hoped I could stay for it.

I expressed my regrets.

But I would stay tonight?

Oh, yes. But then I would have to go on my way. This thing with Fernando did not look good, and I had to try to find out where he might have gone astray.

Alfonso said they had not the slightest idea. At first they thought he took a long time to leave, and then when the boy came, it was evident that Fernando had started out but had been held up somewhere. With the favor of God I would find out something.

I hoped so, I said. I did not know Fernando very well, but Chanate was a good friend of mine, as was Quico his nephew, and others.

Enrique asked if I had any idea at all about where Fernando had traveled.

I explained that he had certainly spent a night in Seneca and that he might have gotten as far as Raven Springs. A man in that town thought he might have seen such a man passing through, but now it seemed as if that was a mistake. I could not account for Fernando having gone through that town, but he may have arrived at the entrance of it. I was going to have to go back and find out.

So you just stay the one night.

Yes.

At that point Enrique said something to Alfonso about a letter. Alfonso got up from his seat and rummaged around at the edge of the lamplight. Then he came back with a white object, which he handed to me.

It was a sheet of paper folded and sealed into the shape of an envelope, and it had my name spelled correctly on the outside. I broke it open and read the brief message.

It was from Magdalena, in Spanish. She would like me to know that she was in Rawlins, at a hotel called the Overland. She planned to be there four days, and it would be quite agreeable if I could pass by there, should I receive the message in good time. I looked at the date on the letter. It looked as if I was going back to Rawlins first thing in the morning.

CHAPTER ELEVEN

The town of Rawlins took on a different personality, gave me a different impression from the one I had formed the day before. Now that I had a sense of Magdalena being there, the place seemed not so harsh. It still did not have an air of benevolence, as I understood it to be the future site of the state penitentiary, but today I could imagine it as a town where not all the women had to peek out through the corner of a curtained window and where not all the children hanged puppies for play.

I found Magdalena without any trouble. A squinting clerk went up the stairs of the Overland Hotel and came back down, soon followed by the most pleasing sight I had had in days. Magdalena wore a gray-blue dress with a matching jacket, the latter bordered with dark needlework. Her hair hung loose upon her shoulders, and as she reached the bottom step I saw that she was wearing earrings of a translucent red stone, either garnet or ruby. She held forth her two hands and, with her green eyes sparkling, greeted me in Spanish.

"Hello, Yimi. How are you?"

Her hands were warm and alive as I took them, and I caught the soft smell of perfume. "Fine, fine, Nena. And you?"

"Also fine."

"And how did you get here?"

"I came on the train from Denver, through Cheyenne."

"You didn't get bored, waiting in this place?"

"It was not so bad. I was able to rest."

I looked around and saw two chairs, each with thin leather padding and a hundred brass tacks. "Let's sit down," I said, "and you can let me know what brings you here."

I held her chair for her and then turned mine so that it was close and at a right angle. She smiled as I sat down.

"Tell me, then. Are your aunt and uncle all right?"

"Oh, yes, thanks to God."

"And everything else? I imagine it is for some reason that you came all this way."

"I have news. A small thing, perhaps, but my uncle thought it might help you to know."

"Very well."

"The first thing is, that it is said that Fernando came to this town. Carrying the Virgin. My uncle heard it by letter."

"Not from Alfonso and Enrique, at the sheep camp. I was just there, of course, where they gave me your letter. They said they had not seen Fernando nor heard a thing."

"It was someone else. Benito, don Mauricio's son, talked to other people when he came here."

"And they think they saw Fernando pass through, with a bundle?"

"Yes. I believe so."

I frowned. "I heard the same thing, and I came this far to find out it is probably a mistake."

She shifted in her chair. "A mistake? In what way?"

"Everyone is focused on the bundle. There was another man, tall and dark like Fernando, who came through on horseback with a package behind his saddle. When people hear the story, they make what they have seen fit what they have heard. And it is understandable, because the Virgin is important. But I don't think Fernando came this far."

Nena took in a quick breath. "Really?"

"I have talked to several people, and that is my conclusion so far." I smiled at her. "That does not mean, however, that you have made your trip in vain. I'm happy to see you."

"Oh, yes. And I am, too. Besides, that was not the only news."

"Oh? What else?"

She glanced around the lobby. "There came a fat man looking for you, a little after you left. The next day."

"A fat man? What did he want?"

"He said he knew you, that he met you with Tome."

"Oh, yes," I said. "I remember. His last name is Entwistle."

She drew her brows together, as in warning.

"Very well, the fat man." I knew that the words *el gordo* would float on the air much less conspicuously than a name pronounced in English. "And what did he want with poor Yimi?"

She smiled. "He was looking for the man who came to talk to you and my uncle. The one who looks for people."

"Oh, yes. The man with the bad eye." Now I frowned as I thought back. "It seems to me that the fat man said he had not heard of that other man."

"Apparently he knew something and wanted to know more. He wanted to know if you knew why the man with the bad eye was going to be traveling between Laramie and Rawlins."

I shrugged. "He had many motives. A wallet full of missing persons. And I didn't know he was going to be traveling that way, although I did see him later."

"Here in Rawlins?"

"No, earlier. In a couple of other places." I thought I detected a trace of worry, so I added, "Why do you ask?"

"Because I saw the fat man here. Yesterday."

"In this hotel?"

"No. On the street. I don't think he noticed me or recognized me."

Now I understood why she looked around the lobby even when she was about to speak of him in Spanish. "Well, who knows. But if he thinks he's going to find the man with the bad eye, he will be disappointed."

"Why is that?"

I then gave her a summary of the main events I had been through, from the time I saw Milaham in Fort Collins until shortly before I left Raven Springs.

"Oh, such people," she said as I came to a pause in the story. "And you think they kill travelers? Just to rob them?"

"I think so. Then they have to do away with people who come asking questions. I don't know for sure that they are the ones, and I think someone else killed the man with the bad eye, but it is very probable that they poisoned the mule driver and his partner before that. Even if I can't find Fernando, I need to go to the law. I just wish I had a little more proof."

"If they have done that much, there is probably much more to be had. You'd like to catch them with their hands in the dough, but it might well be hard to do."

I had to appreciate her phrase. *Con las manos en la masa* has some poetry to it, and it conjures a nice image of a person whose hands are sticky with tortilla dough.

"Yes," I said. "I didn't like to leave, but I had to go out and investigate these other strands, and at least they have shown me that I have to go back there."

I went on to tell her about the rest of my travels, including my visits in Rawlins the day before.

"So you saw this man? Does he look like Fernando?"

"Not really. But with a general description, and people paying attention to the whole idea of the bundle—it is an easy mistake."

"And what would be the purpose of this man having such a package?"

"He buys and sells jewels," I said. "I would guess that he sometimes buys them from obscure sources and then transports them in his own discreet way, in unpredictable movements."

Nena widened her eyes. "Like smuggling?"

"Something like that. He probably had some jewels hidden in the middle of that bag of grain, like some people hide money in their houses—in a bag of coffee or in a mattress."

Her face broke into a smile.

Her expression made me smile as well. "What makes you laugh?" I asked.

"I remembered a story. A funny one."

"Well, tell it. We have time."

"This was a few years ago. You remember my aunt Eusebia, in Colorado Espreen."

"The widow lady."

"Yes, her. Well, before my uncle died, the two of them went to Santa Fe, to see a doctor who was supposed to be able to cure my uncle. Of course he didn't, but my aunt and uncle went with hope. They didn't have any children themselves, so my aunt asked my cousin Tacha to watch the house for her."

I nodded.

"Well, Tacha said the house was very dirty, for my aunt was already very old, so Tacha and two of her sisters and two other cousins cleaned the house. They were all married and had their own houses, but they got together to help. The five nieces swept and mopped and scrubbed, washed all the sheets and blankets, and went so far as to throw out a mattress. It was very old and dirty. Tacha said my uncle must have had it since he first got married, and she didn't think he should be sleeping on it any more if he was so sick. The five nieces put together their money and bought a new mattress."

"That was generous."

"Yes, it was. But when my aunt and uncle returned, my aunt was furious about the mattress. After some ranting she let it be known that she had stuffed about a thousand dollars into that mattress."

"Really?"

"Now the nieces were all in a panic. They couldn't find the mattress where they had thrown it out, in some dumping ground, and they thought they were going to have to get together the money to pay back my aunt." Nena's eyes sparkled as she paused to smile. "Then she told them it was just a joke, that she hadn't hidden any money in the mattress after all."

I laughed.

"But I think she was angry about the mattress anyway, at least at the beginning. Some people don't like to throw out anything. And it must have been a good lesson for my cousins, who were all grown up and had their own families, and who were made to feel like little girls for a while. And plenty worried."

"I should say so. And of course, some people do hide money that way."

"Oh, yes. When the thieves come, sometimes they cut open mattresses and pillows. They don't care." She smiled again. "But coming back to the story, this man who sells jewels, he didn't have anything to do with anything?"

"I don't think so. He didn't spend the night in Raven Springs. He just rode through, but it was enough for someone to remember, and then it was enough to get me off the track. But I had to come by here anyway, to talk to the man who buys horses and then to go to the sheep camp."

"And now?"

"I plan to go back to Raven Springs, to the last place where I had something definite."

She nodded, and then her face softened. "Shall I go with you?"

My pulse jumped for a second. "I would enjoy the company, but I think it might be dangerous. Those people are not nice."

"We can be careful."

"Why don't we see about the train first?" I said. "For how long do you have your room?"

"I have to vacate at noon."

I looked at the clock behind the desk. It was a little before ten. "Well, let's go and see."

We got up and walked out onto the sidewalk, where the mid-morning sun was warming the store fronts. When we came to the corner where I had turned to find Contreras's office, I wondered what he might have thought about his comments about Mexicans if he had happened to look out the window.

We went down the street and crossed it to reach the train station. Once inside, I saw that the ticket window was closed. I told Nena that if she would like to sit down, I would go through the other door to see if the agent was out by the loading platform. She took a seat on one of the high-backed benches facing the street, and I crossed the station to go outside. I found no one there, but as I came back into the station, I saw a man I recognized. He was sitting at the far end of the wooden bench, on the side facing the tracks. He had his head lowered and seemed to be shading his face, but I knew his portly form and tawdry suit. I thought I should take the opportunity to talk to him.

"Mr. Entwistle," I said as I came within speaking distance.

He looked up and showed a discolored face, more puffy than the other time I had seen it, and it seemed as if he was trying to identify me. "What do you want?"

"I'm Jimmy Clevis," I said. "I met you in the Jack-Deuce, back in Monetta, when you were talking to Tom Devlin."

His eyes roved over me as if he was still trying to place me, and I saw that the white of his left eye was blood-red.

"Oh, yes. You're the one who went looking for the missing Mexican."

"Yes, and I understood you wanted to ask me something."

He gave me a backward wave of the hand. "It doesn't matter."

"Well, it does to me. I'd like to know why you were asking for me."

He shook his head and lowered it so that I couldn't see his eyes, but he didn't look away from me. "It doesn't matter," he said again.

"I thought you told me that day that you didn't know Ross Milaham."

"I didn't, then. I heard about him a little later."

"Do you mind telling me why you were asking for him and me in the same breath?"

"I thought you knew where he was going. I thought you might even be working for him, or with him."

"Not quite."

"So I gathered." He pushed out his lower lip,

which didn't look as moist as it did the day he was drinking beer in the Jack-Deuce but added to his jowly appearance all the same.

"If you don't mind my saying, it looks as if someone has roughed you up."

He raised his head, and I saw the bloodshot eye again. "How perceptive of you."

"What did you think Milaham was?"

He hesitated and then said, "If not a bounty hunter, at least some kind of a detective. Someone who could keep an eye on someone else."

"Frank Contreras?"

A look of resentment came to the battered face. "The man's a bastard."

"He might well be. Did he do it himself, or did he have his thugs do it?"

"He hires out some of his work."

"That's too bad—not that he hires it out, but that it happened to you. Were you expecting him to be picking up some, shall we say, discreet items?"

"Something like that."

"In Denver, perhaps?"

"Who's to say at this point?" He averted his eyes again so that he didn't look at me but didn't look away, either.

"Well, I think he might have transported them sooner than you or your employer might have expected, and I think he may have gotten them here by a different route. You came around through Cheyenne and Laramie, I suppose?"

"I thought you were looking for the Mexican." He had certainly lost the jolly tone of our earlier meeting, but he hadn't lost the ability to talk down to me.

I bounced right back. "I was, but your man rode

right through the middle of my investigation, so I ended up finding out about him anyway. But I don't believe I have any further interest in him."

"Nor do I."

"Nor in any missing persons?"

He shook his head. "I don't know what for."

I nodded. "Good enough, Mr. Entwistle. I'm glad to be able to talk to you, and I wish you a good trip back. Maybe at some better moment in the future, we'll have a drink together."

He gave me an expressionless look and said, "That will be quite the pleasure."

I walked down the length of the bench and around to Nena's side, where I gestured for her to go outside with me.

Out on the sidewalk she said, "What happened, Yimi?"

"I spoke with the fat man."

"Oh, yes? I heard you talking, but I didn't know with whom. What does he say?"

"He was looking for the jewels, and he didn't have any luck. No good luck, anyway. He's going back on the train."

"Oh, Yimi. I don't want to go on the same train. It is a long trip, and he makes my skin crawl."

"Even more now. Some men who work for *el señor* Contreras left his face looking not very pretty."

She took my arm and pressed against it. "Then I can go with you, Yimi?"

I looked up and down the street. "I suppose so. And I imagine there is at least one other person in this town who sells horses." I took the liberty of glancing at her figure. "We also have to get you some riding clothes."

* * *

We rode south of Rawlins, stopping long enough to say hello to Del Scoggin, who was happy to leave off chopping wood and to cast a smiling glance at Nena. Then we went on to Raven Springs. Nena's horse, a dark brown gelding that hadn't been ridden much for a few months, was dog-gentle but needed plenty of nudging. When we tied up in front of the Red Coach Hotel, the brown horse lowered his head as if he was glad to get back to sleep after a short interruption. Nena and I went in to see about lodging.

The Red Coach was a plain establishment with a pale, clean-shaven man in attendance. He turned out to have a bit of a stiff neck, I thought, as he insisted on giving Nena a room on the first floor and me a room on the second. Nena said it was fine, and even though I was disappointed, I didn't have any real objection. Up until now I had kissed her a few times but gone no further, and it looked as if this night was not going to change anything.

When we got our bags into our rooms, I put the horses up in a stable. Then Nena and I sat under an awning of the business next door, a saddle and boot shop that had closed for the day. I told Nena there was a café down the street, and she said she was in no hurry to eat. After another ten minutes I asked her if she would like to go for a walk, as this was the time of day I had seen the old man talking to the man with the bad eye. She said it would be fine.

As we walked down the street I had the feeling that we were being watched, but I didn't see anyone paying attention to us. When we came to the cross street, we turned right and drifted toward Bruno's house. As I scanned the place I saw him out back, moving around like a slow animal and jabbing at weeds with his stick. I whistled like before, and he paused to lean on his staff and turn his head my way. I whistled again and waved, and he turned and came hobbling toward us.

He looked exactly as he had the morning before, with the tight-billed cap, the bristly white hair and stubble, and the cloudy eyes peering ahead as he made his way, doubled over.

"Whatty you want?" he said, which I thought might be his standard greeting.

I walked closer so I wouldn't have to shout, but I was still conscious of talking aloud. "Good evening, Bruno. Do you remember me? I met you yesterday morning. You told me to come back later."

He looked me up and down, then did the same to Nena, who had stayed about a step behind me. "I tink so. You come in the morning. You ask about that other man."

"Not exactly. I said I knew him."

"But you wanna ask questions. I know that." He wrinkled his nose, and I saw the purple edges on his nostrils.

"Someone told me you know a lot."

"I don't know nawthing. Just a stupid old man."

"I know. That's what you said before. But I know you're not. And you told me to come back some other day."

He shook his hand in the air. "No boddy care for me until they want sawm thing. I know that."

"You're a wise man," I said. "I'm the one who's young and stupid."

He gave me a cunning smile. "You gotta pretty woman."

"She's a friend. We're looking for a friend of hers."

"Anawther woman?"

"No, a man."

"Wahl, you stupid all right. And I don't know nawthing."

I could smell his old man odor, and I tried not to breathe in too deep. "I know you know a lot of things. Maybe not about the person we're looking for. But even if you told us something else, like what you told the one-eyed man, that might help us find what we're looking for."

His yellow stumps of teeth showed, and little bits of spit flew out as his voice raised. "I know what you want, and I could tahl you sawm thing. But not today."

My spirit sank. "That's what you said before, so I came back now."

He stared at me with his bleary eyes. "You young and stupid, yah. And you gotta pretty woman. You wanna know what old Bruno knows. Maybe this thing, maybe that." His head wavered back and forth, and he reminded me again of an old dog.

"If there's anything I can do for you, or get for you, I'd be glad to."

"Wahl, you right about one thing."

"That I'm young and stupid?"

"That too."

"I'm not sure what else."

"I could tahl you sawm thing," he said. "But not today. I tahl you sawm awther day." He shifted his weight on the stick, then waved me away with his free hand. "You go on, now."

"Thank you, Bruno. I'll see you again."

I turned away and raised my eyebrows at Nena.

As we walked to the street, she said in Spanish, "Poor old man. He seems to know something, though."

"It's a way he can be important, and he wants to make it last. I can't begrudge him that. And he went a little farther than he did last time. I think he's disposed to tell me something. We just have to wait."

"*Pobrecito.* He must be very lonely. Does he not have any family?"

"I don't know. He said he used to be a baker, a long time ago."

"Well, I hope he helps you."

"So do I. We can try again tomorrow."

As we walked back out onto the main street, I had the feeling again of being watched, but I did not see a face peering out of any window.

That night, when I had gotten Magdalena safely lodged under the watchful eye of the stiff-necked clerk and had gone to my room upstairs, I had a hard time sleeping. Usually I sleep without much trouble, but this time I tossed and turned. For one thing, I had a lumpy mattress, probably older and not much cleaner than the one that Magdalena's cousins threw out. For another thing, I had time to think about how people fared when they went snooping into things.

From appearances, Grimes got a dose of arsenic or strychnine, and Milaham got a knife in the back. Entwistle got a good drubbing. I tried to find differences between what they did and what I was doing, but I could not find enough. Maybe I had been more cautious than Grimes and more tactful than Entwistle. I was sure Milaham had done more than just talk to Bruno in order to end up where he did, and I suspected his motives might not have been the cleanest. But I knew that when someone came too close to a dangerous truth, the party being threatened didn't worry too much about how pure the inquisitive person's motives were.

The idea of getting stabbed in the back was becoming all too real to me. I could imagine sitting in a gentleman's library, drinking brandy and talking about how the truth was worth going after regardless of the trouble it took. And then as I hovered in my thoughts I could look down on myself, squirming on an old deformed mattress and wondering if I would even get to decide how much it was worth.

CHAPTER TWELVE

In the clear light of day, as I was having breakfast with Magdalena in the café, the world did not seem like such an ominous place. We were down the street from the hotel, so I was cut loose from any connection I had with this town. I did not have to worry about whether someone in the kitchen was going to lace our food or whether someone in the stable was hammering the frogs on Little Blackie.

Nena and I had hotcakes with chokecherry syrup and took our time over a second cup of coffee. As we talked, we went around a little bit about whether she would go along with me to the two inns. I argued that it would be exposing her to danger, and she argued that it would be much harder for innkeepers to do something in broad daylight if there were two people present. That made sense, especially after the shuddering I had felt the night before. And as for Nena's delicacy, I wasn't very worried about that. She had seen me in a couple of tight spots before.

We settled on a plan in which we would keep our

rooms at the Red Coach, get the horses out of the stable, and ride down to the inns. We would visit the Gridleys first and then see what we could find out across the way.

I was tying the horses to the rail in front of the Empire Inn when the front door creaked open and Mr. Gridley appeared. He stepped out onto the porch.

"Well, well," he said, wiping his hands down along the length of his stomach. "Back already. What a surprise."

"I hardly left."

"I didn't think you could have rounded up all the horses in the Red Desert that quick."

"Still got that to do."

I lifted my gaze and got my first view of his face. He was freshly shaven below the mustache and side whiskers, and he had a meaty look to his lower cheeks and the underside of his chin. The bags on his lower eyelids made him a bit pig-eyed as well. I was able to take him in like that because he had finished with me and was studying Nena—not in the way that a fellow like Del Scoggin would look her over, with a glow of appreciation softening his face, but rather in the way that an old long-tusked boar would look at a milk cow that wandered through the gate.

He must have caught me watching him, for his face relaxed and he put on a smile as he turned to me again. "Did you run off and get married, Jimmy?"

"No, I didn't, though it wouldn't be the worst thing I could do. This is my friend, Magdalena. She got to missin' me, so she took off on her own and came this way. She caught up with me yesterday. I told her I was expectin' to have to rough it and she'd be better off stayin' in a town."

"Can't argue with that. The only thing is, we can't take in any guests right now."

"Oh." I caught a movement in back of him, and then I saw Norma's hard eyes peering at Nena.

"You see," Mr. Gridley went on, "we're gettin' ready to do some paintin', and we're scrapin' all the walls. Place is pretty unsightly right now."

"Oh, that's all right." I gave a toss of the head. "She wanted to put up in town, where everything was closer, so we got rooms in the Red Coach last night. She plans to stay there while I go out on my work."

"I see." His flat blue eyes moved back and forth, taking her in and then settling on me again.

"But she'd like to find some work to do. Help out with the costs, and give her something to keep her busy."

"We don't need any help," he said right away. "Even when we're open for business, we've got all the help we need to clean the rooms and run the kitchen. And now with this painting, of course we'll do that ourselves, too. We'll have it done in a week. We just have to do it when the weather's still warm, so we can keep the windows open and ventilate things." He twisted his mouth so that the side-whiskers went out of parallel. "Nope, we're a pretty self-sufficient bunch. I'm sure you noticed that."

"I didn't think it would hurt to ask."

"No harm," he said, with a reassuring shake of the head.

"Well, good enough." I took in a breath. "We'll not keep you from your work."

"No trouble. Always good to see you." He turned to Magdalena and gave her a kind smile. "And nice to meet you."

"Yes," she said in English, "very nice to meet you, too."

Mr. Gridley seemed poised, waiting for us to go.

I spoke again. "I hope it's all right if we leave the horses here for a couple of minutes while we go ask at the Falconer House." I waved my head in the direction of the lodge.

"Oh, I'm sure they don't need anybody either."

I wrinkled my nose. "We've got time. Will the horses be all right here?"

"Oh, sure, sure. Go ahead."

Before I turned to leave, I took another glance at Norma, standing in the dark doorway behind the smiling landlord. The sullenness I had sensed before seemed more forward now, like malice. As Nena and I walked away, I could feel the two pairs of eyes upon us.

Across the road, I paused at the door for a few seconds and listened. I could hear no sounds from within. I opened the heavy door, again without the expected creak, and let Nena go in first. I followed close behind and then stood next to her in the silent company of the mounted birds. I looked at the great horned owl, who held his perch in quiet dignity, and I thought I would like to ask him what he knew. It was only a passing fancy, though. I let my gaze rove across the other birds in their various postures, all with their sharp beaks and claws. I gave Nena a minute to absorb the display, and then I touched her on the elbow and directed her attention to the goshawk on the wall behind us. Her eyes opened wide. I had told her about this collection, but seeing them for oneself had to be much more vivid than just being told that the birds were there.

I called out as I had done on my earlier visit, and then I went to the registration desk and knocked on the counter. Not a sound came from the rest of the house. I stepped back to stand by Nena again, then turned to look at the interior. I saw the wall clock, the fireplace, the leather chairs, and the double doors that I presumed would lead into a dining room. I pictured again the layout as I had imagined it from the outside. Still I heard no sounds, no voices, no steps on a wooden floor.

I signaled to Magdalena that I would be right back. With light steps I crossed the sitting area to the double doors, where I took a deep breath before I tried the two knobs. They both turned at my light pressure, and the doors opened toward me. Sure enough, a dark dining room lay within. I stepped inside and saw a door on the left end. Presuming that it went into the kitchen, I moved toward it and pushed it open.

The kitchen also sat in silence, all neat and tidy and unused. Just inside and to my left I saw another door. I crossed the corner of the kitchen, opened that door, and found myself in a short, narrow hallway. I followed it until it ended at a door, where I paused to listen before I opened it.

I identified the room as the proprietor's office. In the middle sat a heavy oak desk, facing the door. In back of it, a bookcase occupied almost the entire wall. Along the right wall, beneath a curtained window, a work table held a typewriter, a stack of loosely arranged papers, and a lamp. The wall in back of me, which would have separated the office from the kitchen, held a set of cabinets. I turned the other way, taking in again the desk and the bookcase, and settled on the left side of the office. Two chairs sat with a hat-and-coat rack standing between them. I turned again to study the other two walls, the ones that held the bookcase and then the window, and I compared what I saw with the layout I had in my mind. I was pretty sure there was another room behind the bookcase, but I saw no door leading to it.

I walked around the desk and let my eyes wander across the spines of all the books on the shelves. Nothing spoke out to me. All the books had a drab, dusty, unused appearance. I wondered if anything, like a photograph or a document, lay hidden inside one of those thick volumes. I wished I had more time to check.

I also wondered what might lurk beyond the bookcase. My heartbeat had picked up, and I knew I had only a few seconds. I looked in back of me to be sure I was alone in the room, and then I searched the left end of the bookcase. On the middle shelf, behind a gray volume of Euclid, I found the latch. I pulled back on it, felt it give, heard a click, and pulled the heavy bookcase toward me an inch.

I paused again, for I thought I heard a noise. Sure enough, it sounded as if someone had come in through the rear of the building. I pushed the bookcase back into place, heard the click, and made my way out of the dark office. Down the short hallway, across the corner of the kitchen, and through the dining room, I was just closing the double doors behind me when the door opened behind the reception desk. Mr. Frye stepped into view and moved his gaze from Magdalena to me as I walked past the fireplace toward him.

"Good morning," he said, then smiled to show his gleaming teeth.

"How do you do?" I answered. "Did you hear me calling?"

He shook his head. "No, I didn't."

I stopped next to Magdalena. "Well, I called once from the desk here, and then I stuck my head in the dining room and called there."

"I see." The dark brown eyes traveled over me. "Do I know you?"

"Name's Jimmy Clevis," I said. "I was in here a few days ago, just admirin' your place. I was staying across the way."

"Oh, yes. Looking for stray horses, I think you said."

"That's right." I put my arm around Magdalena's shoulders. "This is a lady friend of mine. She came out to be closer to me as I do my work. She's staying up at town."

He gave her a quick glance, with a little more appraisal, I thought, than Mr. Gridley had done. "How do you do?" he asked.

"Very well," answered Nena, again in English. "This is a beautiful place."

"Thank you."

"Magdalena is looking for work," I said. "Kitchen work, room cleaning. Something to keep her busy while I'm out on the range."

He smiled, showing his teeth again. "Is that right?"

"Oh, yes," she answered. "I am verry good cook."

His eyes lingered on her. "I bet you are. But I'll tell you." He turned to look at me. "Things are slow. I've had very few guests for several months now. I can't afford to take on any help." He reached into his coat, took out the leather cigarette case, opened it, and held it forward in offering.

"No, thank you," I said, and Nena repeated.

He lifted out a tailor-made cigarette for himself, folded the case, and put it away. Then he reached under the counter, came out with a match, and lit his cigarette. "Before long," he said, "we'll be going into the cold part of the year, when I have even fewer travelers."

"You manage to stay open, though," I said.

"So far. But sometimes I shut up for a month or two in the winter. I'm afraid the people across the road are getting most of the business, even in fair weather."

"Actually," I said, "there might be a little windfall for you right now."

"Is that right?"

"From what I understand. Just a little while ago, Mr. Gridley—that's the owner—told me they had to close up for a while to get some painting done inside."

"Indeed." With the side of his index finger he brushed down on his full mustache.

"Of course, I can't speak for them. But that's what I was told."

"Interesting." He blew a stream of cigarette smoke out through his nose. Looking at Nena, he raised his eyebrows and said, "So you're staying in town, then?"

"Yes."

"Well, you can always drop by again in a few days. If things change and I get busy, I may need some help."

"Oh, verry good," she said.

His eyes came back to me. "And I wish you all the best of luck, of course, in your search for wild horses."

"Not wild horses as much as strays, but thank you."

"Of course."

I took Magdalena's arm, and we turned and headed for the door, leaving Mr. Frye and his perfect head of hair in a haze of smoke. I glanced up at the goshawk in his fierce pose, then reached for the door and opened it. Nena and I stepped out into the daylight.

"What did you see?" she asked me in Spanish.

I waited until we reached the edge of the road, and then I said, "I found his office. First the dining room, then the kitchen, and a little hallway. Inside his office I found a bookshelf, full of books, and behind it there seems to be another room. But I didn't have time to go in. I heard footsteps. Did he come through the hallway from the back?"

"It sounded like it. He barely appeared when you did."

"So I think that's as much as we can do for now. It's evident that no one wants to let us ask very many questions. We can go back to the old man, and maybe from him we can think of more questions to ask." I turned to Nena so that my eyes met hers, and I tipped my head backwards toward the lodge. "All very gracious, isn't he? Do you think he wears a wig?"

She smiled. "It looks very perfect."

"Well, here are the horses. I don't think we need to take leave of the owners, though I'm sure they'll be glad to see us gone."

Back in town, we found a little commotion going on in the yard in front of Bruno's house. A man who looked as if he might be a storekeeper was talking to two housewives, one of whom called to a little boy and told him to stay away from the house. Nena and I dismounted, and she stood with the horses as I walked forward.

The man with the clean shirt and tie looked my way. "Yes, sir?"

"I was wondering if Mr. Bruno might be at home."

His eyes narrowed on me. "Do you know him?"

"I had some questions to ask him, but he told me to come back later."

"You don't say." He seemed to appraise me. "And who might you be?"

"My name is Jimmy Clevis. I'm staying at the Red Coach Hotel."

"And if it's not too much to ask, what kinds of questions did you want to ask Mr. Bruno, as you call him?"

"They concern a missing person. I was given to understand that Mr. Bruno knows a great deal."

"It's too bad you didn't get your questions answered," said the man. "It might help us answer one."

"Oh, really? What's that?"

"Old Bruno was found dead in his backyard this morning. One of the neighbor ladies saw him lying on the ground."

I felt a sinking of the spirits. "I'm sorry to hear that. Had he been hurt at all?"

The man gave me a stern look. "He didn't have any wounds, if that's what you mean. But he was white around the mouth, as if he had been trying to spit something up."

My own stomach felt as if it had a pound of cold iron in it. "That doesn't sound good."

"Not at all. And if you talked to him recently, you might have been one of the last people to see him alive. You say you're staying at the Red Coach?"

"Yes, my friend and I both." I nodded in the direction of Nena and the horses.

"Well, I recommend you not leave town right away. Someone is going to have some questions."

"I should think so."

Feeling dismissed, I walked back to join Magdalena and to tell her what I had found out.

"Poor old man," she said. "Do you think they got to him?"

"Yes, I think so. And now it's more in the public view. I think our friends might feel the net drawing in before long. They have already closed the door on us. I think it will occur to someone to start asking questions at the inn. When they do, our friends are going to be as hard as a rock."

"What can we do?"

"I don't think it will do us any good to sit and wait. I think we should try to find out more while we can. For one thing, I'd like to look inside that secret room."

"How do we do that?"

"I think the man with the wig is there alone. In both visits, he was the only one I saw."

"But if the others are getting worried, won't he be on his guard as well?"

"I think they all are, always. But sooner or later he will have to go to the little house, and when he does, we might try our luck."

"Don't you think he just went?"

"Very possible. But unless one is sitting in a stage-coach, one has to go from time to time."

She nodded. On our trip from Rawlins we had stopped twice where the brush was high.

"Let's try it," I said. "We'll find a place where we can watch, and if we get fed up after an hour or two, we can try something else."

In less than an hour from the time we settled in behind a screen of sagebrush, as I sat in idle thought about how they were going to get Bruno straightened out to fit in a coffin, the back door of the Falconer House opened and the man with the perfect hair came out. I waited for him to get settled into the outhouse, and then, hoping he was there on serious business, I led the horses into view and helped Nena mount up.

A minute later, we stopped at the front door of the lodge. "Better to do things in plain view for the moment," I said, handing her my reins. "If I'm not back in ten minutes, go to town and tell someone."

I walked into the silent front room, waited a second beneath the glassy stare of the two falcons that flanked the doorway that Mr. Frye had come through each time, and headed for the double doors. In another minute I stood inside the office with the bookcase and curtained window. I scanned the bookshelves and found them as before, with all the volumes in place, and no empty spots. Then I found the latch and pulled the section of wall toward me.

The room inside had a curtained window but no door in sight. This would be a tight place if a fellow had to get out of it on short notice. In the dim light I took soft steps forward, moving to my right to go around a couch with a raised headrest, and then, on a low dresser against the back wall, I found something that gave me pause.

The Virgin, a light blue statuette with a tiara or diadem of golden wire, stood about a foot tall. I moved closer to see what thing it was that hung around the figurine's neck and reached almost to the hem of her dress. In the faint light I could not be sure, but it looked very much like a necklace of artificial diamonds with a garnet brooch or pendant.

I let out a long, low breath, and thinking of Milaham, I turned to look behind me. I was still alone in the room, and I knew I had to get out. Then I heard the noise I had heard earlier in the day, the sound of the back door.

I went to the window and tried it, but it was either nailed or painted shut. Just as well, I thought. I needed to close the bookcase.

Inside the office, as the footfalls went down the hall, I closed the section of wall, wincing at the click, and moved to the window. It gave, and less than a minute later I was standing outside, settling the sash in place. Again I looked in back of me, then took off on a fast walk toward the front of the lodge.

I had just cleared the corner of the building and was matching glances with Magdalena, who had dismounted to hold the two horses, when the front door of the lodge opened.

Mr. Frye stepped out. "What are you doing here now?" he asked, with a less congenial tone than before.

"I'll tell you, Mr. Frye." I took a couple of steps forward so that I would be closer to both him and Nena. "I'm looking for a missing person."

His eyebrows went up. "Are you, indeed?"

"Yes, and after thinking it over, I've decided to tell you straight out." I motioned with my head toward the Empire Inn. "I didn't feel I could be that forthcoming with the people across the way."

"Interesting," he said, narrowing his dark eyes on me. "Do you think you can tell me the person's name?"

With great effort I kept myself from looking at Nena. "Yes," I said. "His name is Roderick Entwistle. He's a large, fat man who wears a suit. He tries to give the impression of being neat and jolly, but he doesn't do well at either."

Mr. Frye gave a thoughtful look. "Sure doesn't sound familiar, but as I told you earlier, not many travelers have stopped with me." He frowned. "No, it doesn't ring a bell at all. But I wouldn't be afraid to ask the people over there. They might be low-class, but I don't think they would do anything to you just for asking."

"Thank you, Mr. Frye. I'm sorry for any trouble."

He smiled, showing his teeth. "None at all." Then he looked at Nena and smiled again, with his mouth closed. "*Buenas tardes,*" he said.

As Nena and I walked across the road, she asked me in Spanish, "Is it afternoon yet?"

I looked at the sun. "I don't think so, but it doesn't lack much."

On the other side of the road, we tied the horses at the hitch rack, then sat on the porch of the Empire Inn. I didn't hear any noise inside—not any scraping of the walls, though I didn't expect to—and I didn't smell any paint.

"I don't know how much we fooled him," I said in Spanish. "But as long as he doesn't know how much I know, he doesn't have a reason to do much."

"Did you find out something?"

My eyes met hers. "I saw the Virgin."

She gasped. "*Yimi!*"

"Yes, and without mentioning any name, I think it tells us that the person we are looking for is no longer alive."

"*Pobrecito.*"

"It was a possibility all along. But that doesn't make it easy."

"*Pobrecito,*" she said again. "*Que Dios le ayude.*" Poor man. May God help him.

I nodded, and then after a respectful pause I said, "What we've got to do is think of the right way to break this thing open."

"Then why are we sitting here?"

"My idea is that as long as we sit here, the man with the wig can't come over and tell these people or ask them anything. As soon as I can think out the details of a plan, we'll move."

A couple of minutes later, the front door opened. Mr. Gridley stepped halfway out the doorway. "Well, hello there. I thought I heard someone."

"Been up and down the way, lookin' for work," I

said. "Hope you don't mind us sittin' in the shade
for a few minutes."

"Not at all. Make yourselves comfortable." He
gave a broad smile to both of us and stepped back
inside.

We sat there without speaking for several minutes
as I tried to think of a way to blow the case open. I
still had the deep-down feeling that if I just went to
the sheriff and spilled my guts, these people would
tighten up and it would be hard to get enough on
them. There was evidence, to be sure, but the Virgin
and the necklace didn't connect with Grimes and
Milaham, at least not enough to put anyone's hands
in the dough. I thought that the ideal maneuver
would be to bring someone out, on either side of the
road, but I needed to think of a way that wouldn't
get me killed.

I thought we were in a good spot, out in the open
like that and keeping Mr. Frye somewhat pinned
down, but I wished I had my six-gun on me. Earlier
in the day I had stashed it in my saddlebag, so as not
to give anyone alarm as I pretended to make innocent inquiries. From where I sat I could see my saddlebags, but I thought it would be way too obvious if
I walked over to my horse and strapped on my gun.

As I sat there mulling things over and not making
much progress, the door opened and the girl Penny
appeared. She was carrying two plates of food, and
Ollie followed behind with a plate of biscuits.

Penny stood in front of Nena and me and handed
a plate to each of us. "Norma sent this out," said the
girl. "There's too much food in the kitchen, and
some of it like the eggs is bound to spoil unless we

use it up. Norma told me to tell you that, so you wouldn't think there was any charge."

I studied my plate as I took it. Three strips of bacon sat next to a mound of fluffy eggs. "Why, thank you, Penny," I said. "Tell Norma we appreciate it." I turned to Ollie. "If you don't mind holding that plate another minute, we'll get situated."

Penny walked away, giving us a backward glance. When she had gone inside, I made a wide-eyed expression at Nena, who gave a short nod.

"I'll tell you, Ollie," I said. "We just ate before we came here, but we don't want to hurt Norma's feelings. How about you and me just sneak this out to the dog?" I motioned for Nena to scrape her plate onto mine, which she did, and then I put the four wide, shallow biscuits on top.

Nena said, "Are you going to throw away the bread like that?"

"Sure," I said.

"Will you break it up first, please?"

I nodded. I knew of that custom, of not throwing out a whole tortilla or slice of bread without breaking it into pieces. It had to do with their whole idea of the host, the bread and the wine and all that. I didn't like the idea of touching the biscuits any more than I already had, but I didn't want to go against some article of faith that Nena held.

"Let's go," I said to Ollie, and I followed him around the other side of the building.

The mongrel-looking dog came into view and came toward us, holding its head to one side as if it expected to be smacked. I knelt down and broke each of the biscuits into at least four pieces as the dog wolfed down the bacon and eggs. It pained me to do it. If the eggs weren't laced with arsenic or strychnine, I was wasting some good food. If the food was poisoned, as I highly suspected, I was killing this dog in a thrice. I figured I would know in less than half an hour.

I carried the plate and fork back to the porch and set them by the door with the other tableware.

"Did you give it to the dog?" Nena asked, still in Spanish.

"Yes."

"Pobrecito."

Ollie said, "Her mouth moves different when she talks."

"That's because she speaks Spanish," I said. "You've seen Mexican people before, haven't you?"

He gave me his blank stare. "I guess."

"Go ahead and sit down," I said, pointing at the board floor as I took my seat next to Nena. "Maybe you'll think of a story to tell us."

I sat back in my chair and made a slow turn with my head to see if anything was moving at the Falconer House. At that moment I saw the hag Jeanette taking the girl Penny across the street. They must have gone out the back door. Jeanette had the girl by the elbow, as she had on the earlier occasion when I saw them headed that way. On the surface it did not look that harmful, but in light of what I had seen in the last hour, it made my body tighten in contempt.

CHAPTER THIRTEEN

I nudged Magdalena to draw her attention to Jeanette and the girl. "That's the sister," I said. Then, still in Spanish, I used a phrase that I had heard Nena herself use. "To me it is repugnant," I said, "to know that the man takes advantage of young girls."

"Is that what he does?"

"It looks like it. These people act as if they don't know each other, but there's the proof that they work together."

Nena's eyes had a hard cast to them. "I didn't like the way he looked at me, but it's not that unusual for men to do that. But a young girl—that is very low."

A few minutes later, I heard a ragged sound from around the corner of the building. It sounded as if the dog was beginning to hack and retch. Ollie got up and went in that direction. He came back in a couple of minutes and stood at the foot of the steps.

"What's the matter, Ollie?" I asked.

"I think he's sick."

"That's too bad."

"But the dog's sick."

"Well, I'm sorry."

His eyes started to brim with tears. "You did it."

I got up and went to crouch on the stairs, to keep him from raising a ruckus. "Look," I told him in a soft voice, "sometimes dogs eat their food too fast. You saw how he bolted it down."

The boy gave me a resentful look, then turned and went back in the direction of the gagging noise.

I took my seat and tried to get my mind onto the track of staging some course of action. I gazed at the horse and saw the saddlebags again, and I wished I had my pistol on me. Then I observed the rifle butt sticking out of its scabbard, so close but out of reach. I might have been able to do something when I was hunkered down talking to Ollie, but I hadn't thought of it at that moment. *Fool*, I told myself.

I sat there in silence for a few more minutes, feeling strangely paralyzed and not able to think of my next move.

The front door of the inn opened, and there, to my surprise, stood Jeanette. Her sudden appearance seemed out of place, and as I tried to make sense of it, I figured she must have come back while I was talking to the boy and had my back to the road. She stuck her head past the door frame, made a whispering sound, and motioned for me to come near. Because she caught me off guard, and because I didn't want to risk her saying something suggestive in front of Nena, I got up from my chair and walked over to the door. When I got there, she stepped back and aside, and there stood Mr. Gridley with a double-barreled shotgun pointed at my mid-section.

"Step inside," he said. "I think you know what this thing can do."

Fool, I told myself again. *Damn fool*. But I didn't have much choice. Without a word or a gesture to Nena, I stepped into the front room of the inn.

Mr. Gridley kept me covered as he moved backwards. "Keep coming," he said.

When I was clear of the door, Jeanette closed it behind me.

"Well, Jimmy," said the innkeeper, "I think you can guess your little game is up."

"What game?"

"Oh, come on. What game, indeed. You were no more looking for stray horses than I was. You came here to snoop, and you're still doing it. Having that Mexican girl show up made it all the more evident."

"How's that?"

"Bad. That's how it is."

"Well, then, I'll tell you what I'm up to. I'm looking for a fat man in a shabby suit, a fella who acts like a jolly comrade but is a double-crosser. We were supposed to go fifty-fifty on some jewels, but I think he made off with the whole swag. I'd like to find him."

"Interesting story, Jimmy. You should try telling it to Bruno."

"Is that your strong suit, knocking off crippled old men?"

"We had a soft spot for him. But he ate too much dessert." Mr. Gridley motioned with the shotgun. "C'mon. Down the hall."

I went ahead of him, down the hallway that I was familiar with. I noted my former room as I passed it, then stopped at the door that led outside.

"Go ahead," came the voice from behind. "We're going to the stable. I'll be right in back of you, so I assume you know better than to try anything."

I did as I was told. I stepped outside, crossed the short distance to the stable, and opened the creaking door. Inside, Tim Holman was leaning on a pitchfork and smoking one of his hand-made cigarettes.

I looked around and took in as much of the interior as I could. I had been in the stable a few times before, but now I had a great interest in every item and detail. I made note of the horse collar, the harness leather, the odds and ends of chain, the singletree. I also saw something I hadn't noticed before—a hook hanging from a rafter. It was made of five-eighths-inch iron and was about a foot long, with one end hooked over the rafter and the free end suspended for hanging a lantern or something such. I had seen pairs of hooks like that for hanging a lamb or deer carcass or a quarter of beef, and I could see that this one was moveable.

"Get a rope," said Mr. Gridley.

Tim walked over to the pile of hay and stuck the pitchfork into it while Mr. Gridley closed the door behind him. I had my back to him, but with the creaking of the hinges and the closing off of the shaft of sunlight, I could tell what he was up to.

"Turn around," he said.

As I did, I saw Tim pulling a loose and tangled hemp rope out of the grain box. I imagined they were going to tie me up, and from that I supposed Mr. Gridley didn't want to touch off a shot in the middle of the day. Since he didn't have recourse to his usual method of poisoning, he had to resort to something he was less accustomed to. All of these thoughts passed through me in an instant, along with the assumption that neither of these two men was up to stabbing me in the back or else one of them would have done it already. They wanted to do something quiet and hold me until later. Still, I had a great deal of respect for the double-barreled shotgun.

Tim stood about a yard away from me, scrunching his nose and squinting at the cigarette smoke as he sorted out the tangles of rope. Mr. Gridley, off to my right between me and the door, cleared his throat and made a grunting sound.

All of a sudden the door swung open with a fast creak of the hinges, and daylight flooded in. Mr. Gridley stepped back and around so that the door was on his left and I was on his right.

At first it seemed as if no one stood in the doorway, and then I looked down and saw Ollie.

He gazed up at the innkeeper, who would have been the boy's idea of absolute authority. "The dog's sick," he announced.

Mr. Gridley waved the shotgun. "Get out of here," he snapped. "Close the door."

"But he's—"

"Get the hell out of here!" Mr. Gridley took his left hand off the shotgun and waved it at the boy as he hollered.

I saw my moment and stepped forward, swinging my best punch at Tim's jaw. He raised his head at that instant, and my fist landed on his throat. He staggered back and swooned, falling into the loose hay. I jumped over him and grabbed the pitchfork, scrambling so that Mr. Gridley would have a hard time picking me up as he came around with the shotgun.

He made a silhouette against the open doorway,

so I couldn't see his face very well, but I could tell he was trying to get lined up on me. I swung around with the pitchfork and sent it straight at him with the tines headed for the middle of his body.

He fended it off with the shotgun, but I could tell the fork had jabbed his left hand, for he pulled it up and away and let the shotgun fall to the floor. When it hit, one barrel fired, and the blast sent a barrage of dirt and pellets toward the stalls.

Mr. Gridley stood back, holding his injured left hand. The pitchfork lay at his feet, with the shotgun just beyond it. I went rushing at him, hoping to land a couple of good blows before he could get his hands on either weapon, but in the time that it took me to cover those few yards, he leaned over the pitchfork and got his hands on the shotgun. He had his right side to me and was still bent over when I came at him and smashed my fist against his cheekbone.

The shotgun went off a second time, digging another trench and rattling birdshot against the posts and planks. Mr. Gridley fell over on his side, covering the head of the pitchfork, as I stumbled to my left. Then he surprised me by coming up and around, quick, with the pitchfork in both hands as he blocked the doorway.

I skipped into the open area between the haystack and the stalls. Looking around, I wished I had jumped the other way and gotten my hands on the singletree, but it was too late for that now. I reached up and pushed on the rafter hook, dislodging it, then fumbled to keep it from rapping me on the head or falling on the floor.

Mr. Gridley, meanwhile, had pulled the door shut

RAVEN SPRINGS201

and was coming at me with the pitchfork. I shifted the piece of iron in my hand so that I held it by the end that had hooked over the rafter. Mr. Gridley came bearing down on me, not fast but steady, holding the pitchfork level at me and moving it back and forth. Right away I felt outreached. My own weapon was a little longer than the head of the fork, and that was it.

I started backing in a circle, careful not to cross my feet as I stepped. When I thought I had the rhythm of both of our movements, I swung out with the hook. I failed to grab the shank of the fork, and the end of my iron glanced off the springy metal. I circled a few more steps and tried again, then again. On about my fourth or fifth try, Mr. Gridley thrust the tool forward, and this time I hooked my iron around the shank of the pitchfork where it met the main beam.

He pulled, and I twisted. He pushed forward and yanked back, shook the fork toward me, then hauled back again. With both hands on the handle and quite a bit more weight behind the pull, he got the best of me and ripped the iron hook out of my hand.

When I lost resistance, though, the pitchfork went up higher than his shoulders, and I took advantage of the opening. I drove right at him, planting my shoulder in the pit of his stomach, at the top of his belly where his ribs met his breastbone.

He let out a *whoosh* of air and stepped back, then tried to smash me on the head with the tool handle as he held it crossways. It glanced off my scalp, and I reached up and got both my hands on it as well. Then I hooked my heel behind his, pushed with my hands on the fork handle, and sent him to the floor. When he hit, I followed up with a knee in the middle of his girth, close to the spot where I had driven my shoulder. He let out another gasp and groan, and I wrested the pitchfork from his grasp and tossed it aside, but he wasn't done. With a burst of force, he flailed and thrashed like a roped bear, spilling me off to one side. He rolled to the other, coming up on all fours as I got to my feet.

I saw his eyes go to the hook, which lay on the dirt floor about five feet from his left hand. I sidestepped, nudged the iron hook with my boot, and bent to pick it up. As I did, he pushed up from the floor and came charging at me, bent over. I swung the iron up and around and down, whacking him behind the ear. The blow kept him from rising up, but it didn't stop him. I stepped back and aside, then came around with another swing. This time I caught him with the flat of the hook at the base of the skull. He slumped like a pole-axed steer.

I stepped back and shook my head. A wave of dizziness passed over me, and I had to fight for a deep breath to stay on my feet. As I was doing that, Tim rose up from the hay, ghostly pale, and bolted for the door.

I stood for another moment, trying to collect myself. The daylight pouring in from the stable door helped me remember the world outside. Nena was out there somewhere, as were Norma, Jeanette, and Mr. Frye. Tim was like a fish let back into the water.

I looked around the stable and found my hat where it had fallen early in the fight. As I put it on, my eyes lit on the shotgun. It was useless now, with no more shells. My pistol and rifle were both on my horse. I thought of Nena again, as I had left her on the porch. The others would have gotten their hands on her by now.

My second wind came fast. I tried to keep a sense of caution as I dashed out of the stable and ran along the side of the hotel. I had to jump over the dog, which was sprawled out and still heaving. I didn't see Ollie anywhere. I supposed that after two blasts from the shotgun he took cover.

I stopped at the corner of the building. I heard nothing. As I peeked around I saw the two horses standing as before, and then the empty porch came into view. I ran for the horse, and not wanting to lose time by unbuckling the saddle bag, unrolling my gunbelt, and putting it on, I pulled my rifle from the scabbard and turned toward the front of the inn.

The door stood gaping open. I took three careful steps across the porch, then paused at the doorway. Still I heard nothing. I walked inside and stood by the entryway to the dining room. The premises were silent.

I made a quick tour of the kitchen, the store room, and the hallway. All the guest rooms were locked, and I heard no sound behind any of the doors. I took the stairs two at a time and searched the upstairs, where a couple of rooms were unlocked but had no one in them. The whole place had an odd, mute tone to it. I felt that there was no one anywhere in the building and that I was losing time.

Down the front stairs I went bounding. I paused again by the dining room, then rushed out the front door and hooked left toward the Falconer House.

I ran across the road in the bright daylight, and a minute later I stood in the dark interior with the rigid, glassy-eyed birds mounted along the walls. I was sure there was a quicker way to get to Mr. Frye's office, but I took the route I knew. I had no time to tiptoe, but I tried not to thump as I hurried through the dining room and kitchen, both empty and quiet, then down the hall and into the office.

The end of the bookcase stood out from the wall. No one was in the office, but I assumed that anyone in the secret chamber would have heard me coming. Holding the rifle level and pointed forward, I walked toward the back wall. I stood as close to the wall as I could and poked the rifle barrel through the opening, then eased the bookcase outward. I expected a blast of gunfire, but all I heard was the creak of the hinges.

By now my eyes were adjusted to the dim interior, so as I inched my way toward the opening, I searched the room beyond. Somebody was lying on the couch. I stepped into the chamber and saw the girl Penny. She was wearing her underclothes, and her dress lay draped on a footstool. I tapped her on the shoulder. She stirred and mumbled, but she seemed too doped to talk, and I didn't want to speak out loud unless I had to.

I walked further into the room, and on the other side of a low table I saw something I had missed a moment earlier when I was looking in. A human form lay face down. Coming closer, I saw that it was Norma, arms flung out and head turned to the side. A stiletto handle stood out from between two white apron straps that had absorbed some of the spreading red stain.

Nothing shocked me at that moment—I had a lot to take in, and I had to try to keep my wits about me. I looked around the room, trying to determine what there was to observe. I didn't see the Virgin where it had been before, on the low dresser against the back wall. Near that spot I saw a book sitting by itself.

The girl moved, and I stepped close to see if I could get any sense out of her.

"Penny," I said, leaning over and trying not to speak out loud.

She mumbled something, but I could make nothing of it.

"Penny," I said again, but I could tell it was no use.

I stood up and listened once more. I was sure Jeanette was hiding somewhere in the building, but the place was a maze to me. I imagined there was a hidden door leading out of the secret room, but I couldn't see any traces of one.

The girl made a sighing sound where she lay, but as I looked closer I could tell she was still groggy.

"Hang on, little sister," I told her. "We're not done yet."

I took another look around the room before I left it. I let my eyes linger on the body on the floor for just a moment, to be sure of who it was. Then I left.

With the rifle in front of me, I started to make a search of the building. I retraced the way I had come in, and within a minute I stood again in the gloomy front area in the company of glass eyes, sharp beaks, and claws.

I crossed the room and headed for the door that led to the hallway. Mr. Frye had come through this door both times I had seen him in here. I stood to

one side as I turned the knob and pushed the door
open. Then I walked down the hall, trying each door
as I passed it, left and right. Toward the end on my
right, I thought I heard some motion inside, but I
could not open the door. I thought that the back of
the room might share a wall with the secret quarters, and I tried to picture the layout in my mind.

I stood there, listening for movement in the room,
when I was startled by something much louder than
I expected. It was the scream of a woman, and it
sounded as if it came from outside.

I ran for the back door, pulled it open, and looked
out. I saw a struggle going on near the woodpile.
Right away I recognized Nena by her dark hair and
her tan riding clothes, but I did not know the man
who had a dark arm around her waist and was trying to cover her mouth. It was a man in a clean,
black suit, a man with a gleaming bald head that
bobbed around as he wrestled with his captive in
the sunlight.

Then I placed him—Mr. Frye with his toupee
fallen off. I raised my rifle and got a rest on the door
jamb, then levered in a shell.

Nena shouted in English, "Let me go!" as Mr. Frye
got both arms around her waist. He heaved back,
lifted her off her feet, and slammed her to the
ground. I waited for him to raise up and stand clear,
but he didn't right away. He had one knee on her
and was reaching for something. I thought he might
be trying for a piece of firewood to clobber her with,
but then I saw what it was. He pushed himself up
and away from her and lifted the ax with both
hands.

I did not think much as I drew a bead on his ribs

beneath his lifted arm. For the most part I saw a man who was trying to kill one more person, but in the corner of my mind, somewhat like the corner of my vision, I had a picture of the girl on the couch in the dark room. Then the rest of the world fell away as the bead settled into the notch on the rear sight and I squeezed the trigger.

He flew back, arms sprawling, as the shot crashed and died away. I stood long enough to be sure that one shot had done it, and then I ran into the open to see if Nena was all right.

She was pushing herself up into a sitting position when I got there.

"Yimi!" she said. "Did you shoot?"

"Yes, I did." I crouched down and pointed over my shoulder with my thumb. "I don't regret it a bit."

CHAPTER FOURTEEN

I helped Magdalena to her feet, and as she took a moment to steady herself, I listened. Everything was quiet again, but I figured it was a matter of little time before someone came down from town to find out what the shooting was about.

"That was a bad man," I said, tossing a glance toward the body in the dark suit. "He seems to have killed a woman as well as abusing a girl, and he was getting ready to do some violence to you."

Still in Spanish, Nena said, "Whom did he kill? What woman?"

"Norma," I said, which was easier to say in Spanish than *"la señora Gridley."*

Nena gave me a scornful look. "That was no woman."

"Really?'

"He dragged me across the street to this man's hotel, and when he was holding me with his arms of steel, I could smell him. I tell you, it was no woman."

"Hombre," I said, which I meant more as an expres-

sion of surprise than as a reference to the person in the apron. "Did you see this man stab Norma?"

"No, I didn't see it. After you went into the hotel, Norma and the sister took me over here. The sister held me in a chair while Norma went in to talk to the man."

"Were you in his office?"

"Yes. I could hear them arguing in the next room, and struggling, and then things were quiet. The man came out alone and said something to the sister, and she took off. Then the man twisted my arm and took me outside."

"Through the back door?"

"Yes."

"And you don't know where the ugly sister went?"

"No."

"I would like to know where she is." I studied the exterior of the lodge, thinking she might still be inside somewhere.

"Do you think she's a killer, Yimi?"

"I don't know. It's possible that she didn't kill anyone, but she was certainly an accomplice. She helped Norma and the señor finish off travelers, and she helped this man do dirty things to the girl. I'd like to see her get taken in."

"And the señor—where is he?"

"Mr. Gridley, when I saw him last, was lying face-down on the stable floor. I gave him a pretty good one with a piece of iron." I nodded in the direction of the road, and we started walking. "Here's an idea. I can go into the stable and see about him, and you can stay outside to keep an eye on this place."

Nena took a wide look around. "You're sure Norma won't come?"

"A knife in the back," I said. "Very effective for detaining a person."

I left Nena at the corner of the inn next to the road. Still carrying the rifle, I tried to keep my eye on the back door of the inn and the open door of the stable as I made my approach. Everything was still and quiet. I paused next to the doorway of the stable and listened. Not even a fly buzzed. I inched my way forward until I could see inside.

Mr. Gridley lay as I left him, motionless, sprawled out on his stomach with his face turned away from me. I walked up next to him and poked my rifle barrel at his ribs. He gave no response at all. I knelt and touched his ear, and from the feel of it I thought the warmth was going out of his body. I must have fetched him a pretty good one, all right.

When I rejoined Nena at the corner of the building, she gave me an inquiring look.

"He's finished," I said.

She gave a sigh of relief.

At that moment the front door of the Falconer House opened, and Jeanette came out in a hurry, headed toward the front of the Empire Inn. She was carrying something, holding it close to her. Then I recognized it.

"It's the Virgin," I said in a low voice to Nena.

She gave a short intake of breath as I kept my eye on Jeanette. When the woman stepped into the road, she caught sight of us and started running to the inn. I ran for the front corner of the building to head her off, and she turned to the right in the middle of the road and took off toward town.

I dug in for a stop, leaned my rifle against the building, and turned the other way to run after her.

As I came pounding up behind her, I said, "You might as well stop. Everything's up, and you know it."

"Fook yourself," she huffed, and kept running.

I caught her and grabbed her by the left arm, pulling her around in a half-turn. She came to a jolting stop, then with a vile expression on her face, spit at me. With her left arm pulled against her body to clutch the Virgin, she came around with her right hand and clawed at my face with her fingernails.

I pulled my head back in time and my upper cheek was barely scratched. I grabbed for the figurine, but Jeanette had both hands on it again and held it close. I still had a hold of her arm with my right hand, and with my left I grabbed at her right wrist. She tried to yank free, and I pulled her back. Then she twisted and wrenched, and I jerked. Finally her grasp gave way, and I grabbed at the light-blue object, barely touching it with my fingertips. The Virgin fell on the hard-packed road and broke into a hundred pieces.

Jeanette took off running again, and I stood in a daze. After all the trouble and danger, it had come to this. Part of the Virgin's face stared up at me, and the gold tiara lay cock-eyed in the rubble.

Nena came hurrying toward me, then slowed down for the last few steps. "It's the Virgin," she said.

"Yes, it is. And I feel as if I helped break it."

She shrugged as she looked down at the fragments. "There's nothing we can do about it now."

"Well, it's still evidence," I said, "and we can't leave her in the middle of the road. Do you have a handkerchief?"

She pulled out a bandana the size of a scarf, and the two of us knelt to pick up all the pieces.

"It looks like she scratched you," said Nena.

"She is very disagreeable."

When we had everything but the smallest grains picked up, I tied the corners of the cloth and made a bundle, then held it as I stood up.

"What things these people do," said Nena after she came to her feet and looked around.

"There was no reason to kill for it. It was just a hollow, empty figure—no treasure inside, and no great value in itself, as far as money goes."

We began walking back to the horses. Before we reached the building, the front door opened again on the Falconer House, and the girl Penny stepped out, squinting in the sunlight. She wobbled, unsteady, so Nena and I hurried over to her. She had her clothes on, but in her foggy state she looked as if she was not yet fully awake.

"Be careful," she said in a slurred voice. "Mr. Frye—"

"I know. There's been some trouble." I patted her on the shoulder. "But don't you worry. These people are all under control."

Her face was clouded as her eyes met mine. "I heard a shot. Is Mr. Frye—"

I nodded. "Don't worry. He can't come back at you."

"And Cale?"

"Neither will he. And I suppose you saw Norma."

The girl moved her head up and down, solemn-like.

"Let's go over there," I said, "and let things clear out for a moment."

We crossed the road to the inn and sat on the edge of the porch, where my rifle was not far away and I could see up and down the thoroughfare.

"Where's Ollie?" the girl asked.

"I don't know. I'd guess he's hiding. Mr. Gridley, or Cale, as you call him, tried to do me in, and his shotgun went off a couple of times. I imagine Ollie took cover."

Penny shook her head and widened her soft brown eyes. "You're sure that Cale and Mr. Frye aren't coming back?"

"Yes, I'm very sure."

She let out a breath, and her whole body seemed to sag.

"I know these people did some pretty bad things," I began, "and I don't want to ask you questions that are too personal. But I need to know a few things, just to finish the work that I came here to do."

Her eyes met mine, with an expression that neither resisted nor agreed.

I pointed to the bundle I had set on the floor of the porch. "Those are all the broken pieces of a little statue that Mr. Frye had. I suppose you know which one I mean."

She nodded.

"I've been looking for the man who brought it here. A Mexican man."

She made a faint downward motion with her head.

"I have a hunch that he stayed at one of these two places, probably right here, and he never made it out alive."

Another motion of the head.

"Where did they put the bodies?"

She gave a small shrug.

"They poisoned travelers, didn't they?"

She held her mouth tight and then said, "I guess so."

"Well, they had to do something with the bodies.

Actually, I know where the last two are buried, but I'd like to know where the others are."

Penny shrugged again. "I don't know."

I tried to be patient, but I knew time was wasting. "Try to think. Anything you can say will help."

After a couple of long breaths, she said, "When I first came here, they buried them in the corral. But then they started taking them to other places."

"Tim would know, wouldn't he?"

"I think so. Where is he?"

"Probably hiding somewhere." I took a measured breath as I glanced around. "Did he get rid of the horses and mules, too?"

"I think so."

"He's a good one. I hope someone catches him." I thought for a second. "Let's go back to the man who was carrying the figurine. Why would they want to poison him? He wasn't worth that much."

She delayed for a few seconds, moistening her lips. Then she said, "It was a mistake. They were on the lookout for someone who was supposed to be coming through, carrying some kind of valuables hidden inside of a package."

"Jewels."

"I think so."

"And this man fit the description, and he was carrying a package."

Penny made a very slow up-and-down movement with her head.

"My God," I said. "They killed the wrong goose."

She frowned as she cocked her head.

"Just an expression. I think I know the man they were looking for."

"Oh."

"And how about the other fellow? The man named Lawhorn, whose partner came looking for him."

She nodded.

"Just money on that one."

"Uh-huh."

I let out a sigh. "It didn't seem to bother them very much."

Penny looked at the ground.

I imagined she was thinking about how she had brought us the two plates of food, but I didn't blame her much for that. I was more interested in the people who cooked things up. "So what was their connection with Mr. Frye? They don't seem like very likely partners."

"I don't think they always were. But after Cale and Norma had been here a little while, Mr. Frye figured them out, I think."

"Oh, I see. So they had to give him some of their take."

"Something like that."

"He was here first, then."

"Yes."

I wagged my head from one side to another, weighing a few thoughts. "And what do you know about the necklace? Earlier in the day I saw it draped around the little statue."

The girl's face clouded again as she looked at the ground.

"You know what necklace I'm talking about, don't you?"

She didn't move.

"I'm sorry, Penny. I'm not trying to be nosy, but I

think the necklace used to belong to another girl. Would you know anything about her? A girl named Mary."

Penny shook her head.

"It would have been a few years back. But you know the necklace, don't you?"

After a long moment of silence she said, in a hard voice, "He said it was for pretty girls."

A chill ran through me. "I see. Did he have you wear it sometimes?"

She was moving her head back and forth, but from the way she bit her lip I didn't think she was denying what I said.

"He gave you some kind of dope to make you woozy, didn't he?"

The girl hunched her shoulders, as if she were shivering.

I couldn't see her face, just her straw-colored hair, and I couldn't help thinking how young she was to be going through all this. "I'm sorry it happened to you, Penny, and like I said, I don't mean to be nosy. I'm just trying to figure things out."

She moved her head up and down again.

"Did you know a man named Milaham, a man with a milky eye?"

"No," she said, raising her glance.

"I think he was looking for the girl Mary, and I think it got him a knife in the back."

"I don't know."

"I don't either, but it seems to fit with the way Mr. Frye did things."

The girl went silent again, and I realized that the last few words I said meant something else to her.

"I'm sorry any of this happened," I said. "But if it's

any comfort, I can assure you that all three of these people are beyond ever doing anything again."

A bitter look crossed her face.

"I appreciate you telling me as much as you did."

"It probably doesn't matter."

"Not in the sense that it could change anything, but it can help put together some answers." I held her eyes with mine for a few seconds. "Would you be willing to tell the same things to someone from the law?"

After a couple of seconds she said, "I guess so."

"Good. Because I expect there'll be someone down here before very long."

I looked at the road coming down from town, and it was still empty. After a moment's thought I decided to go see what else I could find in Mr. Frye's chamber. First I needed to be better armed, so I fetched the rifle, walked around the front of the building, and put the gun back in its scabbard. I dug into the saddle-bag, pulled out my gunbelt, and strapped it on. After giving Blackie a pat on the neck, I went back to where Magdalena and Penny sat on the edge of the porch.

"I'm going to go take another look in the lodge," I said. "I hope you don't mind waiting here with Magdalena."

The girl turned, and I could tell she was put at ease by Nena's smile, but neither of them said anything.

I crossed the road under the bright sun and went into the dark interior of the Falconer House. Pausing to look around, I noticed that the wall clock had stopped. The stuffed birds seemed to be the guardians of a house of death, and I felt as if each of them watched me as I made my passage to the double doors.

Once inside the back room, I tried to study the place, but I felt I wasn't really seeing. Everything appeared to be the same as before, still and shadowy. Norma hadn't moved. I went over all the objects again—the couch, the stool, the table, the dresser. Then something clicked. The book that had been lying on the dresser was no longer there.

Jeanette had come back into the room. She had left with the Virgin when I came in, and then when I went running out of the building after Nena screamed, she had come in and done something with the book.

Quick now, I thought. That book had some connection with the necklace, and I could barely remember what it looked like. Just a normal book, drab-colored, common cloth binding, not a part of a leather bound set or anything like that.

I hurried to the other room, the office, and scanned the bookcase. I guessed there were somewhere between a hundred and fifty and two hundred books, most of them plain and common. Of the five shelves, I decided to start on the second one down. I flipped through the pages of one book after another, not skipping any, not even those with binding I was sure didn't match the book I had seen on the dresser. I expected a letter or a photograph or a newspaper clipping to flutter out from one of them, but book after book had nothing but printed pages. In several books, the pages had not been cut yet.

I went all the way through the first shelf and started on the second. The dust was starting to tickle my nostrils, but I kept at it, trying not to lose a minute. Book after book, I riffled the musty pages.

Then, a little over halfway through the middle shelf, a book that looked no different than a hundred others fell open like a jewelry box in my hands. The book had been hollowed out, and the inner edges of the pages had been glued together. Inside, I found something that stopped me cold.

Four locks of hair, each one tied in thread, lay like miniature corpses in the secret box. One lock was dark brown, two were common brown but not the same, and one was a light blond. Mr. Frye the collector. I imagined he had it planned that when he was done with Penny, a lock of her straw-colored hair would go in here, too.

That still left the necklace. I set the book on the desk and went through every other book in the case, and I failed to turn up anything more. The necklace had been here in these rooms somewhere. I reasoned that when Norma and Jeanette came to ring the alarm, there had been a hurry to do something with the various bits of evidence, and there had been a struggle over some part of it. Mr. Frye must have taken the book out, intending to do something with it, and then he got interrupted, probably in an argument about the necklace. Jeanette took the Virgin, hid with it until she heard the shot, then came back through and put the book in its place on the shelf.

I went back into the secret chamber. I examined the floor, looking for a trap door with a brass ring handle, pressing the wall for another hidden door, searching the ceiling for a hatchway. Then I stepped on something.

Kneeling by the couch, I pulled the thing into view and picked it up. It was a necklace, and I

guessed that the little stones were imitation diamonds. But the brooch or pendant was gone. I supposed that in the struggle, after the brooch had been
torn off, someone had tossed the necklace aside.

I turned and gazed down at Norma. Until that
moment I had managed not to think about what
Magdalena had said about the person in the apron
smelling like a man, but now the thought crept
through me. Norma was no longer just an object on
the floor, something to be stepped around, but the
remnants of a forceful person—a murderer, an accomplice, a blackmailer, and things I didn't have a
name for.

As I stood there, chilled, I didn't like where I was.
I felt I had been in the building way too long. Even if
Mr. Frye was dead, which I was sure he was, this
was a room where girls were smothered and adults
were stabbed in the back.

I gathered the necklace into my hand, picked up
the book, and got the hell out of that place. When I
walked out into the sunlight, two men on horseback
were talking to Nena and Penny.

The man in charge of the sheriff's office and the jail
was a lean, angular deputy sheriff who seemed to
resent the idea that someone had done something
wrong in his town. As the afternoon wore on, he
went back and forth between his office and my win-
dowless cell, where I answered questions from time
to time about the deaths of Cale Gridley and Samuel
Frye. I gathered that Jeanette made me out to be a
rampaging murderer, so I had a ways to go to justify
what I had done. From the nature of the deputy's
questions, I formed the impression that he had

Jeanette in one place and the girl Penny in another. Jeanette wasn't talking about anything but my attack, as it was described to me, but apparently the girl answered questions and made the deputy glad he had Jeanette in custody.

He still kept me locked up, though, and he didn't seem to trust my motives for having the necklace and the hollowed-out book. I think he had too many things to put together, and he didn't want me to tell him how to do it. I wanted to know where the missing garnet was, and he was still trying to nail down Jeanette as the person who brought the custard to Bruno.

This last detail came to me through friendly conversation with the jailer. He was a droll, balding fellow of about forty, the type who found all gossip interesting and most of it humorous.

"Yup," he said, picking at his teeth with a toothpick he had just sharpened. "Old Bruno talked too much. I don't know if he knew a tenth of what he let on, but he must've known somethin' for them to do 'im that way."

"Poor old man," I said. "I don't think it took much provocation for them to slip someone a spoonful of strychnine. Old Gridley, smiling all along, and there's Norma in the kitchen dealin' out the doses. What's all that hammering, anyway?"

"Oh, the barber next door. He usually keeps one coffin on hand, and they already got Bruno stuffed into it. Now they gotta make three more."

"Lot of work."

"Oh, he's got someone else to do the sawin' and nailin'. He mostly tends to preparin' the bodies, you know."

"Sure."

"I guess he found a little surprise." The jailer pursed his lips and poked them out.

"Is that right?"

"Uh-huh. He sure did. That one that everyone thought was a woman—well, when Jake pulled out the knife and went to put a clean shirt on the body, he saw she didn't have any tits. Just stuffing. And some chest chair." The jailer held up his right hand, with the index finger curved down. "Didn't take much more to find out she had a little peter."

"The hell."

"That's what he says."

"I kind of had a hunch that not everything was on the square with that one." Actually, I hadn't doubted Nena from the beginning, but I played along with the jailer and let him be the news bearer.

"Yeah, and it gives you a whole new way of thinkin' about Gridley himself. Of course they're both dead now, as dead as Romeo and Juliet, laid out side by side next door."

The jailer went back to picking his teeth, and I listened to the rat-a-tat of the hammers. I'd heard of men sitting in their cells and hearing a crew bang together a gallows, and I was glad they weren't doing that for me. But I still didn't like sitting in a jail cell, knowing I wasn't going to get out until someone turned the key.

CHAPTER FIFTEEN

The deputy sheriff seemed to form a new distrust of me when I told him about Grimes and Milaham. He sat next to the bars outside my cell and kept his steely gaze on me.

"You seem to know a hell of a lot, and you seem to get around where dead bodies turn up."

"That might be," I said. "But from what that girl says, there's been a lot more bodies than I've seen." I didn't mention that it had all been going on under his nose for years. I just added, "If you get a hold of that stable man, you'd have someone who knows everything I stumbled onto, and a lot more."

"We're working on it."

"And I wish someone could find the pendant that was on that necklace."

"I don't know why you're so interested in that little jewel."

I was starting to feel impatient with the sheriff, and I didn't want to be talking down to him, but I gave it to him straight. "Look at it this way. You've got someone poisoning and robbing travelers on one side of the road, and you've got someone using and disposing of young girls on the other side. The parties are in cahoots, and they're trying to hold something over one another."

"You've got proof for some of that, but a lot of it is just theory."

"Well, you've probably heard of that Dr. McCabe, in Seneca, who lost his little girl."

"Oh, sure. Everyone has."

"I think he could identify that necklace, and I think he could tell you which lock of hair belonged to his daughter. More than that, he could identify the stone. It was a garnet that belonged to his mother."

"We searched both rooms."

"I suppose you did, and I wouldn't expect it to have gone anywhere else, unless Jeanette had it. I'd guess it got torn off the necklace right toward the end, and no one had the time to go hide it somewhere."

"So you're saying I should search Jeanette."

"Not necessarily, but if you do, you want to remember that a woman can hide things like jewels in a place that a man can't."

After a stone-faced second or two, he said, "But you think she has it."

"No, I think Norma does."

"Norma? The freak? Why, that one's a—"

"I know. So you're not going to find it where a woman might hide it."

"So what do you mean?"

"I think Norma might have swallowed it. You could get the barber to make a small opening and find out."

"Swallowed it?"

"To get leverage on Frye. Why else would he stab an accomplice in the back?"

"You seem to know a lot about how these kind of people think."

"I believe I know more than I want to, and certainly more than I set out for. But like I said, if you can get that stable man to talk—"

The sheriff stood up, lean and stern. "We're workin' on it."

"When do you think I can get out of here?"

He finally smiled. "If the barber doesn't find anything in the body, we might need someone to search the Gridley woman. Jeanette." He rested his hand on the butt of his pistol and walked out.

Later that afternoon, the jailer showed up looking as if he had heard a good joke.

"What's new?" I asked.

"I guess they found the pennant in what's-her-name's gullet."

"Norma?"

"That's the one."

"How about Tim, the stable man?"

"They're out looking for him."

"The deputy sheriff?"

"No, he's still trying to get something out of the Gridley woman, but she's tight as a clam."

"I shouldn't wonder. How about the girl?"

"He's still got her in a room, but she's just about talked out."

"She's given him plenty to go on, though."

The jailer widened his eyes. "Oh, yeh. Enough to hang a regiment of 'em."

"And he's talked to Magdalena, my friend."

"Sure. He got a statement from her quite a while ago. He just can't get the old bitch to crack."

About an hour later, when I could still see daylight through the window in the opposite cell, the jailer wandered in again. He had his ring of keys to jingle, but he didn't look as if he was going to let me out. He stood a couple of yards away.

"Anything new?" I asked.

"They caught Holman and dragged him in. He was hiding in the stable here in town, waiting for the dark so he could go back and get some of the boss's money, then get a horse. Stevens wouldn't give him one on credit, and when the last wave of news went around, Stevens came and told on him."

"What news was that?"

The jailer held up his hand and crooked his index finger downward.

"I doubt that it had much effect on Holman, though."

"Not that in itself. I guess he tried to be tough at first, but then they showed him the three bodies, and that softened him up."

"Huh. How about the girl?"

"They let her go free. I think they got enough from her for the time being."

"So they might get some information out of this Holman. Do you think I could talk to the deputy sheriff?"

"What for?" He wiggled the key ring and made it jingle.

"I'd like to know two things—how the dentist's

little girl got here, and where Fernando Molina Valdés is buried."

The jailer rolled his toothpick from one side of his mouth to another. "I can pass that on."

Daylight was starting to fade when the jailer came back and stood next to my cell. "I got one answer out of two. Holman says he don't know nothin' about the girl. It must have been before his time."

"Well, I'd bet anything it was her. Is anyone going to notify Dr. McCabe that they might have turned up something?"

"I think the sheriff'll send word."

"I hope so. And what about the other question?"

The man shrugged. "As for your Mexican friend, he was one of a couple of bodies they burned. Knocked down an old shack and had a hell of a fire."

"They just didn't care, did they? And they sold all the horses to that fellow Sloan over in Rawlins. Not a damn thing left, even if the man had a family."

The jailer lifted his ring of keys and fitted one of them into the lock on my door. "The way Holman makes it sound, Frye was the worst of the bunch." The latch clicked, and the door swung open. "I think he's still stickin' up for the boss."

"Might be." I picked up my hat and put it on. "Am I free to go, then?"

"Yep."

"That sounds fine to me."

As I stepped through the open door, he said, "You know what was the best thing you did in this town?"

I shrugged. "I'd say it was telling the deputy sheriff where to look for the pendant."

"That's one view. I'd say it was stickin' the knife between that she-man's shoulder blades."

I flinched. "I didn't do that. Frye did."

The jailer laughed. "I know. I was trying to make you say which one deserved it more, Gridley or Frye."

"I don't know. I didn't really choose to do either of those things. There was no other way."

The jailer cocked his head. "You're not sayin'."

"I'll just say I'd pull the trigger again."

Magdalena was waiting for me in the lobby of the Red Coach Hotel. She stood up and held her hands out for me to take.

"I knew they would let you go free," she said, in Spanish as always. "Just a question of when."

"The sheriff took a while to catch up."

"And they're still holding the sister?"

"Oh, yes. And the man who worked in the stable. They let the girl go. Have you seen her?"

"No. Do you think she went back to the inn?"

"She might have, to look for her brother. What do you say if we go down there on foot. You put the horses away, didn't you?"

"Oh, yes. Like you told me."

"Good. Shall we go, then?"

"Aren't you hungry?"

"Not yet."

She took my arm, and we walked out onto the street. The sun had set, and long shadows lay across the town and the landscape beyond.

When we got to the edge of town, I saw a brightness up ahead. Light flickered in the dusk, as if there were a fire in front of one of the inns. As we walked further, flames began to show on both sides of the road. Then the odor reached us—not the clean smell of firewood, but the mixed smell of different materials burning together, as when someone burned a heap of rags, scrap wood, and moldy paper. I stopped, thinking it was a bit late to try to do anything and it would be just as well to let the two buildings burn. I imagined there was more evidence going up in smoke, especially in the Falconer House, and I was sorry to think of the owl being consumed by the flames, but for all the other bad things the place had inside it, I was content to stand there and watch.

"The girl?" said Nena.

"I imagine so, with the help of her little brother."

The next morning, as the stench of the smoking ruins hung in the air, the word around town was that the two kids were nowhere to be found. I took that as a good sign. Penny would have had the foresight not to let the money go up in flames with everything else. Much better that she should use it than Holman. How she and her brother got away did not worry me much, but what would become of them after what they had been through gave me a more uneasy thought. I could not forget the way Penny hung her head or the way Ollie gave his blank stare.

Nena and I did not ride past the charred remains on our way out of town. Instead, we rode south and around, and when we reached a high spot on the other side, we stopped the horses and looked back.

There on the plain lay the black scar of the two buildings, with wisps of smoke still rising.

"It's too bad," said Nena, "that there are so many people in the world that a person cannot trust."

"Yes, and sometimes I wonder why I find myself in their company. Maybe it's because I used to be one among them."

"Try not to worry about the past, Yimi. You did what you set out to do on this trip."

"I think I still have to tell the bad news to the dentist who lost his daughter. Even if the sheriff should get around to it, I told the doctor I would tell him. I don't look forward to it, but I think I should."

"You see how you keep your word? That's honest. Try to put all the other things behind you."

"I suppose so. Maybe if we get far enough away from this place, we can get rid of it. I know a town where we can bathe in the mineral springs, eat and drink without worry, and sleep in a clean bed. It's called Warm Springs."

"Always the good ideas, Yimi. I hope you are not in a hurry."

Her smile lifted my spirits. "Not once we get there," I said. Then I touched the spur to Little Blackie, and Nena and I were on our way across the plains.

THE RELUCTANT ASSASSIN

PRESTON DARBY

Legends Never Die…

What if John Wilkes Booth escaped? Is it possible the most famous assassin in U.S. history became a fugitive in the West? That's exactly what one man comes to believe after finding Booth's long-lost journal. A fascinating and lively storyteller, Booth details everything from scouting for General Custer to rustling up trouble with Doc Holliday. And in his own voice, the former stage actor and master of disguise recounts how the greatest regret of his life led to an adventure beyond his wildest dreams.

TODHUNTER BALLARD

LOST GOLD

A Deal With the Devil

Bill Drake has been a murderer and a cutthroat all his life. Even his gang doesn't quite trust him. Yet Mary Thorne knows he's the only hope she's got to find the treasure her grandfather buried in the heart of the Superstition Mountains. She also knows Drake could kill her anytime. Or the vicious Apaches who want the loot for themselves could murder them all. Yet Mary has more tricks up her sleeve than Drake thinks. It will take a cutthroat to beat a cutthroat if Mary wants to claim her share of the gold and stay alive.

BIG IKE

ANDREW J. FENADY

The odds have always been against Big Ike. When he risks everything to start a new life in the gold fields of California. When he joins the Union Army and is wounded leading a charge at Shiloh. And now he faces the greatest odds of his life, as he leads a wagon train through hostile Apache territory to establish a freight line in Arizona.

He has a gentle nun on one side of him, a reformed prostitute on the other—and a notorious gunman on his trail, a hired gun who has killed many men before…and who is now paid to kill Big Ike.